THE BASKERVILLE PAPERS

A Dark Sherlock Holmes Murder Mystery

Kelvin I. Jones

CUNNING CRIME BOOKS

The Baskerville Papers

All Rights Reserved. The right of Kelvin I. Jones to be identified as the author of this book has been asserted by him in accordance with the Copyright, Designs and Patents Act of 1988. No reproduction, copy or transmission of this publication may be made without written permission. First published 2016. Note: All references to or utterances of historical characters in this novel are purely fictional.

Chapter 1

In the summer of 2015, the discovery of my great aunt's battered despatch box, found in the dusty attic of her little cottage near Birling Gap, marked the beginning of what would prove to be a bizarre and extraordinary investigation. Previously, I had always been led to believe that Sherlock Holmes was a fictional, though admittedly mythical figure, created by that literary lion, Sir Arthur Conan Doyle. But the discovery of what I later came to term 'The Baskerville Papers' was to change my opinion utterly.

Let me explain. My name is James Perry. I was raised in Scotland - in a small village in Fife, to be precise. My mother's folks were all Hudsons, an old Edinburgh family. About 1875, my great uncle Jimmy, reputed to be an alcoholic, emigrated to London, where he ran a successful pub in Cheapside. When he died unexpectedly from an aneurysm at the age of thirty, his wife Martha suddenly found herself the recipient of her husband's equity. She decided to purchase a profitable bed and breakfast business, situated in Baker Street - then a fashionable part of the metropolis - and there she remained for some forty odd years. In the November of 1880, she was struck by a hansom cab, sustaining two fractured legs, and remained in St Barts Hospital for six weeks. On her recovery, she decided she would lighten her working duties by renting out the first floor flat of her establishment. On the first of January, she was introduced two prospective tenants, one of these being a retired army surgeon, the other, his friend, a consulting detective.

I recall little of my Aunt Martha, apart from a few fleeting recollections of walking with her and my mother along a huge chalk cliff, which I can only assume must have been somewhere around Beachey Head. Also, the beehives in her back garden which she tended and one summer's day when I approached too closely and was stung for my pains. Among my mother's effects, there is also an old photograph showing my mother, looking remarkably youthful. She stands outside a flint - capped cottage. Beside her is me at the tender age of six, and a plump, red faced woman in her seventies, wearing a tartan shawl. I can also distinctly recall a visit to the village church in Cuckmere Haven where Aunt Martha sang in a loud soprano voice.

Aunt Martha passed away in the summer of 1938 when I was a skinny eight year old. My mother and I had moved to Caernarvon in Wales to avoid the bombing in London, my father being at sea, fighting for King and Country. It was not until 1972, when I had finally grown weary of a teaching career, that I got to visit the little cottage in the Downs. My mother had died, following a long and painful battle with cancer, I was quite alone in the world and somewhat depressed about my future.

The name of the cottage, 'The Apiary', should have sent a message to me, but it didn't. So should the name Hudson, but not being one who reads much fiction, the penny didn't drop. Until, that is, I decided to investigate the attic.

It was a hot summer's day. I had not long arrived from Bermondsey where I had spent more than five years as a secondary state teacher. During those long years I had suffered verbal and physical abuse from a variety of my pupils, who were from many far flung corners of the realm. I had become convinced that the profession I had chosen had proved to be a colossal error which had plunged me into a deep melancholy. When the taxi finally arrived on that sweltering July afternoon at the tiny hamlet of Cuckmere Haven, it felt that I had at last found my redemption.

It truly *was* a haven. The rooms were small but cosy, much smaller than I had remembered as a child. But certain features I did recall: an ornate Victorian fireplace in the lounge, and a narrow flight of stairs leading up to the landing, giving access to two bedrooms, both of which provided quite stunning views of the sea. At the rear of the cottage was a long, well stocked garden with beehives.

The cottage was blissfully quiet but rather musty. Leaving my luggage on the faded sofa, I began to stroll from room to room. The lounge was indeed small and cluttered with furniture, most of it from the 1930's. There was an equally diminutive kitchen, housing a well stocked, deeply recessed larder. I walked up the creaking staircase. At the front of the cottage was the largest of the bedrooms with enough space to accommodate two tall bookcases. I stood for a while, browsing their contents. It was a curious and diverse collection. There was a copy of Winwood Reade's 'The Martyrdom of Man', Thomas Carlyle's 'Sartor Resartus', several handbooks on beekeeping and a copy of 'Criminal Investigation' by Hans Gross as well as several works on chemistry. There was a distinct odour to the room which suggested to me that whoever had resided here had been a heavy smoker. On one wall, adjacent to the door were a series of what looked like bullet holes.

The second room was less cluttered than the first. It had a small bookcase containing mainly fiction and military history. There was a small single bed, a comfortable easy chair set by the casement window, and a collection of day to day diaries. I was about to investigate these when there was a knock on the door below. I went to investigate and found an aged woman on the doorstep, enquiring whether I was settling in, and would I like some fresh laid eggs and home made lemon drink?

As we sat chatting, she told me much about her neighbour Martha, of her generosity and a little about her former lodgers. She never knew their names and rarely saw them, though they had lived with Martha for a number of years. The taller of the two was the beekeeper, but he never spoke to her, whilst the shorter man was more approachable and stockier.

After she had left, I decided I would leave the stack of diaries and inspect the attic. I found a rickety wooden ladder which I took from the garden shed and climbed up.

Opening the trapdoor, I shone my torch over a collection of old chairs, chemistry apparatus, various bric a brac and, at the far end, next to a bird's nest, what appeared to be an old battered metal trunk, with the initials JHW inscribed on its lid. With some difficulty I heaved it past the trapdoor and down the ladder.

Back in the lounge, I cleared the dust from the lid and rummaged through the chest's contents. There were numerous bundles of manuscripts, several of them written in a neat, copperplate hand and again signed JHW. There was also a sheaf of letters from someone called 'A.C. Doyle.' I put these aside and, delving further, came across a black folder, marked with the words: 'Not suitable for publication.' I opened the folder. It consisted of several diaries, official reports and statements, some of which were headed: 'Scotland Yard.'

By the time it had grown dark and I had read most of the contents of the folder I had determined that it was my duty to reveal to the public at large the scandalous and bizarre series of events which I have given the less than sensational title of 'The Baskerville Papers.' The reader may note that I have not doctored these papers nor provided for them my own commentary, but simply arranged them in an order which I hope makes some sort of sense.

James Perry.

January 1st 2016

The Baskerville Affair: Letter to Dr Conan Doyle. September 29th, 1929

Dear Arthur,

First, allow me to commiserate with you. When I telephoned you yesterday, your secretary Mr Wood, informed me that you had been quite out of sorts of late and were on no account to be disturbed. I hope that you are not severely incommoded. I would not have bothered you with this matter at all were it not that my dear friend and colleague Sherlock Holmes is now quite severely ill and has been admitted to the General Hospital at Eastbourne. His doctor informs me that at best he has but a few weeks left to live.

With this in mind, perhaps you will let me explain to you the rather delicate nature of my position.

There is in my possession a collection of papers and assorted manuscripts relating to a case which presented itself to Holmes and me in the first few months of 1901. You will no doubt recall the year well, not least because of the death of our monarch and the accession of her son, to whom Holmes was of much service in the narrative I later penned for The Strand Magazine as 'A Scandal In

Bohemia.'(which first brought Holmes to the attention of the reading public.)

I did not bring this to your attention at the time, since you had, I recall, recently returned from South Africa and was enjoying a short convalescent break at Cromer. The Baskerville Papers, as I have termed them, consist of a number of papers, diaries and memoirs pertaining to the death of Sir Charles Baskerville, whose encounter with a Newfoundland hound I chronicled in late 1888. You were most wise to advise me then of the importance of allowing a gap in time to let the dust settle and I have done much the same with these present papers. Holmes believes now that the public should know the full, unvarnished facts about this appalling affair. For myself, I feel that because the content of the material is so deeply shocking, revealing the worst of human depravity, I am loathe to present it to our usual publisher without severe bowdlerization. I would, therefore, appreciate your opinion of the papers. May I send them to you when you are sufficiently recovered?

Yours,

John H Watson.

The Baskerville Papers: Letter from ACD to Dr John H Watson, 1st October, 1929

My Dear John,

It was wonderful to hear from you after such a long interval. You ask if I have been 'incommoded.' In my case, it is a matter of the spirit being willing, but sadly, the flesh is showing signs of wear and tear! I fear that our regular pilgrimages to foreign lands in an attempt to spread the message about The New Revelation, has finally had its toll. I was informed only two days ago by my doctor that my heart is weak and he has instructed me to rest, but there is so much to do in the cause of Spiritualism and the doubters and sneerers (not least those cynics in the SPR) seem always in the ascendant! Mrs Doyle, of course, has ordered me to rest in bed but, though I feel at times like an aged carthorse carrying a heavy load, I am still eager to take up the sword in these matters.

You mention that our dear friend Sherlock has been ill recently. I am sorry indeed to hear that and, were I not presently 'incommoded', would certainly have driven over to see him. Since that business with the German spy Von Bork, I always believed that Sherlock might have been retained by his brother Mycroft in an advisory role to the Ministry but I suppose that his charismatic nature would preclude such a possibility! Your friend is, I believe, an intellectual colossus. How lucky he has been to find such a faithful and skilled chronicler!

By all means, do send me your collection of papers, etc, to which I shall give my immediate attention.

Yours, ACD.

The Baskerville Papers: Letter from Arthur Conan Doyle to Dr John H Watson, 23rd October 1929

My Dear John,

May I first offer you my sincerest condolences on the death of our friend Sherlock. I was most disappointed that I was not well enough to attend his funeral which I read in The Times was attended by over a hundred friends and admirers. May I say that you gave a most moving ovation. He was not only someone we both admired and respected, but also someone of unique importance who will always be remembered and revered in the world of criminal investigation. As you may recall, I employed many of his methods in the case of the much maligned George Edalji, the presumed horse slayer, (with some success!) and, such is his renown, that not a week goes by when I do not receive letters requesting 'Mr Sherlock Holmes's' assistance in the discovery of missing jewels, or some such thing.

I am informed by my doctor that next week I shall at last be given my freedom and will no longer be consigned to the bedroom. It has been a period of relative tranquility, I must admit. I feel much stronger now and shall miss the view from my bedroom window, which commands a fine view of the beech trees and the little garden where I try to do much of my writing. (I preclude from that the writing of letters, which seems to take up half a morning!)

Nevertheless, I have been warned to 'take it easy', whatever that means! Next week, Mrs Doyle and I will travel to Cardiff to see the psychic George Valentine. He has, some say, a unique ability to produce ectoplasm. We shall how he fares under controlled conditions!

But I digress!

Regarding your 'Baskerville Papers.'

I have read and reread your collection of papers. Their contents are so shocking and the conspiracy revealed so challenging that I am not entirely convinced that the public at large are ready for such revelations. It disturbs me to think that at the end of the 19th Century, such human depravity and evil manifested itself in our society here in England. The 'Baskerville Papers' show a degree of perversity I think I have rarely met elsewhere in the annals of crime. Part of me is persuaded that the papers *should* be placed before the public, that we should publish and be damned, yet there remains that small shadow of doubt in my mind.

Therefore I must only conclude that the decision whether or not to present these papers to the public should remain your own. I am only sorry I cannot be of more assistance in the matter. Perhaps we may see you soon at Windlesham where we can talk at length about the matter. We shall be back from our Welsh travels by the third of November.

Yours ever,

ACD.

The Baskerville Papers: Letter from John Watson to ACD, 3rd of November 1929

My Dear Arthur,

I hope I find you well and refreshed after your trip to Wales. For my own part, it has been a frustrating couple of weeks. On the 24th of October I had the great misfortune to go head over heels down the staircase here at the cottage and in so doing, fractured my left humerus. Fortunately I was rescued by the valiant Mrs Hudson and taken to the Eastbourne General. I have been lucky in one regard: I am right handed, hence the writing of this missive.

Having a great deal of extra time on my hands, I began thinking about our departed friend, Sherlock. His executors have written to me, informing me that I am to be the recipient of all of his books and manuscripts. On Tuesday last, a series of large boxes arrived here. Since frankly there is not room for all of their contents at the cottage, so I wondered whether you might manage to look after them at Undershaw? One of those boxes contains a collection of manuscripts of my own which include accounts of cases Holmes and I shared earlier in his long career. There was the astonishing case of the giant rat of Sumatra, for example, the business of Colonel Warburton's Madness, that bizarre case of the red leech and the awful death of Crosby the banker. There is also a complete set of papers relating to that shocking series of murders which took place in 1888, starting with the appalling death of the Queen's surgeon. (yet another of Holmes' cases for which the world is not yet prepared.)

It occurred to me that you might at some stage in the future choose to turn these small works of mine into the pristinely crafted narratives which frequently appear in The Strand.

Back to the 'Baskerville Papers.' I think that on balance I shall choose not to proceed further with the project. Do you recall that business of the thirteen nude paintings by the novelist, Lawrence, taken from the gallery in Mayfair in July? I fear that by publishing the 'Baskerville Papers' in their unabridged state, I would be invoking a similar opprobrium. Or perhaps I am a creature of timidity and should not be quite so fearful. After all, these documents contain nothing more shocking than the horrors we encountered in The Great War and those crimes against humanity you yourself faced in South Africa and in The Congo.

So there it is. During my recovery I shall continue to edit the papers and annotate them.

I hope to see you and your family before the festive season is upon us once more and may hire a driver to get me to Undershaw (at last!)

Meanwhile, I am ever yours,

With kind regards,

John H Watson.

PS I very much enjoyed reading in The Strand your excellent Professor Challenger story, 'The Disintegration Machine.'

The Baskerville Papers: Letter from ACD to John H Watson, January 16th, 1930

My Dear John,

You must forgive me for not writing back to you earlier. It seems that Old Father Time has again punished me and I am once more confined to my quarters, following our return from Africa. Wood has been answering the bulk of my correspondence, save for the most personal mail. He is a first class secretary.

It was a pleasure to see you on Boxing Day and to find the time among the family revelries to talk about old times. It seems so long ago when we first met at that hotel in London with Greenhough Smith and where poor Oscar Wilde was inspired to write The Picture of Dorian Grey. And for us it was The Sign of Four - or as our American cousins would have it: The Sign of *The* Four. I always thought that I had delineated the personality of Sherlock fairly but, as I recall, you thought otherwise, reminding me sharply that he was 'not a drug addict, rather, one who takes drugs!'

How sad it seems that I should be talking of your dear friend in the past tense. It reminds me that 'They are not long, the days of wine and roses,' as the poet Ernest Dowson once wrote; 'Out of a misty dream, Our path emerges for a while, then closes.'

There. I am growing maudlin! Yet the advance of age and infirmity is anathema to one like me, who has devoted much of his life to the challenges of the physical world, yet I am and always was immersed in the world of mist and shadows.

Talking of which, I must tell you that I have at last thrown in the towel with those cynics at The Society For Psychical Research. They flatly refuse to accept the truth when it is staring them in the face and, frankly, I have grown weary of them. Indeed, I grow weary of the world and must admit that I look forward to inhabiting an altogether happier world where I shall once more be reunited with those who I have lost.

Jean sends her best regards to you and enquires as to the well-being of your industrious bees. How fitting it is that you should take up the gauntlet from dear Sherlock and attend their needs. I always had great faith in Royal Jelly which may not be the elixir of life but comes pretty close to it. As you know, Jean is a very sensitive medium and lately has had some remarkable 'visions', including a nightmare in which a 'dark shadow spread itself across the countries of Europe, led by The Dark Prophet.' If such a vision should prove accurate, I fear for the future of our race.

But these are grim and melancholy thoughts. You were right, by the way, to put the 'papers' to rest, at least for the forseable future.

We should meet up soon. I shall send a car down to Sussex and collect you when this freezing weather relents.

God speed.

Regards, ACD.

Chapter 2

DR WATSON'S JOURNAL

In the year 1901, my friend Sherlock Holmes faced one of the most challenging cases of his long and distinguished career. In the thirty odd years of our association, I cannot think of another case which tested him to the absolute frontier of his immense abilities and at times even threatened to overwhelm him.

The complexity of the affair I have termed 'The Baskerville Papers' was made even more challenging for Holmes because of the involvement of certain prominent members of Moriarty's gang (the professor himself had perished some years ago at the Reichenbach Falls in Meiringen, Switzerland, where he and Holmes fought to retain their footholds.)

It had been a quite remarkable and challenging year. In the summer months of 1901, Holmes was involved with the Abergavenny murders, when a whole family was brutally butchered by an unknown assailant, and their body parts strewn around the family's manor house, a gruesome matter which was only concluded through Holmes' expert understanding of fingerprints (it was only in July that Scotland Yard opened their Fingerprint Bureau, which proved to be a breakthrough in criminal investigation and my colleague was, as usual, ahead of the game. This innovation was largely pioneered by our old friend, Inspector Lestrade.)

This success was swiftly followed by an equally complex case which I later came to describe in 'The Adventure of The Priory School.' As in several of his complex cases, Holmes was employed by a high ranking member of the establishment and his brief was to travel to Derbyshire to find a nobleman's missing son. The outcome of this case was determined by Holmes' astute examination of horse shoes.

On a national front it had been a year of great change. In the early months of the year our much loved monarch passed away and was buried with pomp and circumstance at her beloved Windsor. In the Spring of that year Holmes was visited by a member of our Royal Family on a very delicate matter concerning his son, who, for reasons of discretion, I shall refer to as AV. In 1888, it was rumoured that AV had been discovered at an address in Cleveland Street which was being used as a male brothel. At the subsequent trial of the proprietors of this iniquity, two men, Hammond and Newlove, were charged with procurement for immoral purposes. Then, in 1890 fresh claims were made that AV had been present by Henry Labouchere, a member of the Liberal Party. The young man's solicitor maintained stoutly that his client had been nowhere near the premises.

Also intricately involved in this scandalous affair was Lord Somerset. Somerset was then the head of the Prince of

Wales' stables. Although Somerset was interviewed by police, no immediate action was taken against him, and the authorities were slow to act on the allegations of Somerset's involvement. On 19th of October Somerset fled back to France. Lord Salisbury was later accused of warning Somerset, through someone who had met Lord Salisbury the evening before, that a warrant for his arrest was imminent. This was denied by Lord Salisbury and The Prince of Wales wrote to Lord Salisbury, expressing satisfaction that Somerset had been allowed to leave the country and asking that if Somerset should "ever dare to show his face in England again", he would remain unmolested but Lord Salisbury was also being pressured by the police to prosecute Somerset. On 12th of November, a warrant for Somerset's arrest was finally issued.[By this time, Somerset was already safely abroad, and the warrant caught little public attention. After an unsuccessful search for employment in Turkey, Somerset lived the rest of his life in self-imposed and comfortable exile in the south of France.

The reader may by now have determined the identity of our august visitor who was anxious to silence some of the reports which had appeared in salacious American newspapers regarding AV's sexual proclivities, one even claiming that 'AV's involvement with the Cleveland Street scandal has been yet another indication of the debauchery which affects the present Royal Family.' Holmes' intervention in this affair did much to prevent the Royal Family from slipping into disrepute, though it could do nothing to allay the rumours that surrounded the reputation of his client, who became widely known for his dealings with certain high class courtesans and a chair kept for him in a Parisian bordello.

It was, as I well recall, a wild and windy day in Autumn when the affair of The Baskerville Papers began. I had slept heavily the previous night and when finally I entered our cosy sitting room at 221B, I found that the breakfast things had already been laid. A distraught looking Martha Hudson swept into our room, and, casting a withering look at my companion, who was asleep on the sofa, exclaimed:
'And I don't suppose he'll be wanting any tea or coffee either!'
'You shouldn't concern yourself with him, Mrs Hudson. He'll eat when he feels the need. Those kippers look delicious.'
'They certainly ought to be. Best Arbroath kippers.'

There was a slight noise of a match being struck against the mantle as Holmes, bleary eyed, loomed into view. He was dishevelled, his hair was tousled and he was sporting a week's stubble.
'Forgive me for saying so, my dear fellow, but you look the worse for wear.'
'How very observant of you, doctor. Coffee if you please and no milk. I need to recharge my batteries.'

I dutifully obliged him. Holmes swept a collection of plugs and dottles from the mantle, filled his old briar and tried again to light it. A rank and pervasive stench soon filled the room.

'You have been busy, I take it?'
'I have been doing very little - apart from sorting out the affairs of certain noblemen, an activity I find wearying.'
'You are referring to the problem of AV?'
'That is no longer a problem. It has been resolved. The Press can be an invaluable resource if you know how to manipulate it. Has the seven o'clock post been yet?'
I pointed to the card table. Holmes leapt to his feet and picked up a bundle of letters.
'Bah! Bills, more bills. What's this? 'I believe my husband is having an affair...' And this: 'A large and valuable statue of The Buddha was stolen from the garden of our Kensington villa...' It's an unmitigated bleat, Watson, a rag bag of trivia. Small wonder that I take refuge from this cacophony of inanities in the embrace of Morpheus.'
'So you are still using the morphine?'
'Yes, when I have need of it.'
'You no longer heed the cost?'
'I do not wish to repeat myself, Watson,' he replied testily. 'You know I cannot abide ennui. The morphine is merely an antidote. What else should I do?'
'But consider the risks to your health. The mental deterioration, the weight loss...'
'It is no more harmful than tobacco, no more addictive. The risks are minimal but the euphoria great to combat boredom!'

Holmes paused as there came a loud rap on our front door. Then, in an instant, he leapt athletically from his fireside

chair and bounded down the stairs. He returned, clutching a brown envelope and a small piece of paper.
'Aha!' he exclaimed, his eyes glistening. 'At least now we have some grist to the mill.'
'What is it?'
'A request from our old friend, Inspector Lestrade.'
'Chief Inspector now, so I hear.'
'Quite so. A reward, no doubt, for his sterling work in the fingerprint unit.'
'What does he want?'
'My advice on a murder. Does a trip to Fulham inspire you, Watson?'
'I would be happy to assist you - after breakfast.'
'Carpe diem, carpe diem! Mrs Hudson will keep your kipper warm for you. We leave in ten minutes.'

Parson's Green was a square of grand, stucco pillared villas surrounding a small, tree lined garden which, like the houses overlooking it, had seen better days. A stocky uniformed policeman stood on guard outside, rubbing his hands and exhaling frosty breaths.
'Mr Holmes, Dr Watson,' he nodded to us. 'Chief Inspector's on the first floor, flat three.'
We entered, then climbed up a flight of dingy, brown varnished stairs. A second officer stood on the landing looking bored. As he saw us approaching he straightened up and smiled nervously at Holmes.
'Ah, there you are, Holmes,' said Lestrade, who had appeared in the doorway.
Holmes shook his hand vigorously.
'Congratulations are in order, I believe.'

'Thank you. You've lost some weight since our last encounter, if I am not mistaken.'
'You are correct. I see that you have adopted my methods.'
The Inspector smiled wryly.
'The Bogus Laundry Affair. That must be more than six months back.'
'The body, Lestrade?'
'In here, gentlemen.'

We entered a large room with high, ornately stuccoed ceilings which had been stained a patchy brown from years of incessant tobacco smoke. There was a faint chemical odour. The naked body of a plump, middle aged man lay in a spreadeagled position on a stained rug by the hearthside.
'He was found by a neighbour, a Mrs Gilmore. She lives next door in Flat Two.'
'At what time was that?'
Lestrade glanced down at his notebook.
'About six o'clock this morning. She noticed his front door was open. Got quite a shock when she went to investigate. She heard nothing.'
'Has anyone been in this room since the discovery of the body?'
'Only constable Sims - and myself of course.'
'And you both have touched nothing?'
'Of course not.'
'I'm sorry, I had to ask.'

Holmes glanced about the room. It looked as if burglars had turned it over. Books and papers were strewn across the floor, a lamp had been knocked over and a large mirror

smashed. Holmes went over to the fireplace and carefully poked the ashes with a poker. Then, looking like an industrious bloodhound, he traversed the room, stopping every so often and talking quietly to himself. After some while he went to the body, leaned over it, and began sniffing.
'What is it?' I enquired.
'Can you not tell?'
'I confess, I cannot.'
'An odour not unlike pears. It's Dr Collis's Remedy.'
'Chloral Hydrate. The sleeping remedy.'
'But also a treatment for the symptoms of alcohol abuse. Although an overdose would cause sedation, ataxia, coma, miosis and gastrointestinal problems.'
'Or erosive injuries to the esophageal or gastric mucosa, resulting in hemorrhage or perforation,' I observed
'Thank you, Doctor. It is possible that ephrotoxicity or even proteinuria may have killed him, but that would be mere conjecture.'

Holmes leaned over the corpse again.
'There is something else. A bitter smell. Yes, as I suspected. You may observe the stiffened hands? He has suffered a series of violent convulsions.'
'Strychnine then.'
'Or something similar, although strychnine is still the most popular among our poisoners. You may recall Dr Neill Cream?'
'The Lambeth poisoner?' said Lestrade. 'I was privileged to see that rogue hang at Newgate.'

Holmes said nothing more but continued his minute examination of the body. At last, he stood up.
'What do we know about the identity of this man, Lestrade?'
'His name is Leonard Smith. A publisher of rare books, by occupation. You may know of his reputation.'
'Did he not publish The Yellow Book? I enquired.
'A favourite journal of the bohemian sodomites,' Lestrade observed acidly.
'And a patron of Aubrey Beardsley and Oscar Wilde,' I added.
'Apparently he ran a bookshop just off Kingsway. It specialises in smutty books. The Society For Public Decency tried closing it down.'
'And did they succeed?' Holmes asked.
'They did not. So what do you make of the case, Mr Holmes?'
'I have seen enough here.'
'Suicide then?'
'I think not, Lestrade. Did you not observe the marks on his wrists? The man was first stripped and his wrists were tied. He was then tortured and sodomised before poison was administered. And you say the next door neighbour heard nothing?'
'She seems profoundly deaf.'
'I should like to see her nevertheless. What about the residents of the flat directly above this room?'
'An elderly couple. They heard nothing.'
'Very well.'
'You can assist me then?'

'I believe I do owe you a favour, Lestrade. I shall do what I can, though I fear this may be a complex business.'

Mrs Ada Gilmore, the occupant of flat 2, was a wizened eighty year old. She sat on a pile of tapestried cushions in a room cluttered with carvings of Asiatic and African origin, a large stuffed parrot in a gilded cage, and a large oak dining table bearing two red bowls of waxed fruit. On the wall above her marble fireplace hung the portrait of a bearded man in naval uniform. She picked up a brass ear trumpet and beamed across at us.
'That is a painting of my dear Archibald. He was a naval captain, you know. He died in the Afghan War,' she added ruefully.
'You must miss him dreadfully,' I replied. 'Have you lived here long?'
'These past twenty years. Of course I still have my Bertie.'
'Your Bertie?'
'My African parrot. Archie picked him up in Bombay.'
Holmes smiled.
'Mrs Gilmore, what can you tell me about Mr Smith, your neighbour?'
'He seemed very nice. He used to help carry my shopping up the stairs for me.'
'Did he have many visitors?'
'Quite a few. There was a young man with a pale face and dark hair. He used to visit quite often. Sometimes he came with an older man.'
'Can you describe this older man to me in more detail?'

'Well, let me see. He was much taller than the other man. He had long, shoulder length hair and a chubby face. And he wore a silk brocaded jacket.'
'Any other visitors you can recall?'
'Several young boys. Telegraph boys they were mostly. They used to visit him at all times of the day. Nice looking boys, I thought.'
'In what way?'
'Fair haired, good looking boys. They used to stay there for quite a while. Well mannered, all of them - well brought up, I should say.'
'Yesterday, do you recall if Mr Smith had any visitors?'
'As a matter of fact I do. There were three of them. They came here in the morning.'
'What time would that be?'
'About ten o'clock. I had just got back from the greengrocers.'
'Could you describe them?'
'One of them was quite tall with a thin moustache and pale face. He had very blue eyes.'
'And the other men?'
'The second was small and stocky, rather on the fat side. He was wearing a flat cap and was carrying a bag.'
'What sort of bag? Large or small?'
'More like a Gladstone bag, like the bags the doctors carry.'
'And the third?'
'I don't remember much. I only saw the back of his head. He had his hair in a ponytail.'
Holmes stood up.

'You have been most helpful, Mrs Gilmore. And very observant.'

'It must have come as a shock for you, finding Mr Smith like that,' I observed.

'Come, Watson. We must let Mrs Gilmore have her rest and be on our way.'

'Oh, but it's no problem - you are both welcome to stay. Would you like some tea?'

Holmes declined the offer and we were soon out onto the frosty street looking for a passing cab

Following our return to Baker Street and after a light lunch of ham salad, provided by the ever dutiful Mrs Hudson, Holmes left me to my own devices and I sat by the fire with my after lunch pipe, reading the Times. The lead article carried a piece describing the investiture of the new Prince of Wales, an occasion of much pride to our nation. Browsing through the rest of the paper, I came to the letters section.

One particular letter caught my attention. It read:

'Sir,

I was gratified by seeing a recent report in your newspaper of the suppression of at least one of the many shops which now exist in the metropolis for the sale of obscene works and pictures. How is it that so many more are left unmolested has long been a matter of wonder to me. I would draw your attention especially to Holywell Street and Wych Street, in which are shops, the windows of which display books and pictures of the most disgusting and obscene character, and which are alike loathsome to the eye and offensive to the morals of any person of well regulated mind.

This mischief, however, does not exist solely in these outward displays - that is perhaps the least danger - but, alas, is nothing to the effect such works are calculated to produce on the minds of persons whose morbid desires induce them eagerly to peruse them, often to the destruction of their health, and, infinitely worse, to their souls' danger.

Sincerely,
Major James Hadderly.'

I set to thinking about the man whose body we had seen that morning and of his occupation. It struck me that the real connoisseurs of such literature were not the consumers of lewd prints and photographs, but eminent members of the middle and upper classes. As a member of The Criterion Club, I had had first hand experience of such matters. One evening after our annual dinner, a small group of us had been sitting smoking and drinking together at the bar. One of the members suddenly produced a brown paper envelope and from it tipped out a collection of photographs. They depicted a young, well endowed woman in a number of suggestive poses, which I shall not describe in detail, for fear of offending the sensibilities of my readers. Sufficient to say that the young woman - I shall not use the word 'lady' - was entirely naked.

'Cracking shots!' said one member to another - the latter I knew to be a minister of the cabinet - 'Most enticing. How can we get some more like this?'

'You have to have the right connections,' his companion replied. 'Some of us here are members of a book club. I can provide you with details if you require them.'

'Think I'll take you up on that offer,' said a third, his eyes glistening with anticipation.

At the time I found the incident mildly disturbing, though I could not deny that the subject of the photographs possessed a very fine physique. But to dare to publicise her best features in this brazen way I found to be unacceptable.

Whether it was due to the large breakfast or the warmth of the fire, I think I must have fallen into a deep sleep, for when I awoke, the room was filled with acrid smoke. At first I thought there had been a fire but when I peered through the miasma, I saw the outline of Holmes who was sitting, pipe alight, cross legged on two cushions on the far side of the lounge. Although his eyes were closed, I knew for certain that he was fully awake, utilising that rapier-like mind with which I had grown accustomed over the twenty years of our association.

'I see that you are awake at last, Watson.'

'I gather you have been busy then?' I inquired as I moved across the room to open a window.

'I have been down to Scotland Yard.'

'To see Lestrade?'

'To the new Fingerprint Bureau. Lestrade and his cronies have made good progress with their work. So far, they have catalogued the fingerprints of no less than five thousand criminals.'

Holmes went to the hearthside, took a spill and relit his old brier.
'They really should congratulate themselves. At last, they have understood the basic principle of blood grouping, and adopted the Sherlock Holmes test which I pioneered twenty years ago.'
'What news of the murderer of Leonard Smith?'
'We progress, Watson. Though your description is slightly inaccurate. There were three men in the room when Smith died and this was confirmed by the old neighbour who gave us that brief but useful description. The taller of the three looked on for at least twenty minutes as his confederate tortured Smith, who was gagged. His arms and legs were bound. His injuries were considerable but that was not what killed him.'
'The strychnine?'
'The strychnine. It took another ten minutes before he finally died.'
'How do you know there were three men?'
'Because of the cigar ash: a Havana, whose ash is immediately identifiable from the long, pale striations among the other, darker material. It takes on average twenty minutes to smoke a Havana and there was only a short stub in the hearth, close to where he was standing. The third man did not appear to smoke.'
'Have you formed a theory yet as to the identities of his attackers?'

'Thanks to the Fingerprint Bureau, I have made some progress in that regard. The smaller of the three is Parker, a known garrotter, who some years ago had the misfortune to work for the late Professor Moriarty. You will recall that he spent quite some time watching our rooms here at Baker Street. It turns out that he has just been released from Wandsworth, following his part in that affair.'

I was about to question Holmes further when there was a loud rap on our door. Holmes opened it to find our landlady, clutching a telegram envelope. He opened it and his face clouded.
'What is it?
'Something rather odd, Watson. And not good news. In fact most disturbing news. Beryl Baskerville, Sir Henry's wife, has disappeared.'

Chapter Three

INTERRUPTION

Letter from Sir Richard Burton to Leonard Smith - 10th September, 1883

My Dear Leonard,

It was wonderful to at last set eyes on my translation of The Kama Sashtra which I picked up only yesterday after my return from Trieste. You have made a magnificent job of the book, with its tooled and gilt edged leather binding. As you know, this truly has been a labour of love for me (though not of the carnal variety!) and has occupied a great deal of my time and energy, especially since I had to work from four different manuscripts to eliminate errors. I am anticipating a print run of two hundred and five for members of our society, though it would be judicious to print more in case there is a demand among the usual collectors.

I hear that you have been experiencing some trouble with 'The Society For The Suppression of Vice' recently. I refer to this absurd lobby as 'Mrs Grundy, a woman known for her narrow and dogmatic views about sexuality.

I am currently wrestling with my translation from the Arabic of 'The Scented Garden, which, you may recall, is a manual of erotology. As with the Sashtra, I shall be best served by a private subscription to the work - if, indeed I ever finish the damned thing, my health being what it is. Thank God for chloral hydrate and the blessed laudanum!

I shall be in town next Tuesday and may drop in to see you at the bookshop - that is, if you are not busy.

Regards, Richard.

Letter from Leonard Smith to Sir Richard Burton, 12th September 1883

My Dear Richard,

How good it was hearing from you once more. I can report that the Shastra has proved so popular among our subscribers that I have been persuaded to issue another print run of 500 additional copies. Ashbee, one of our best supporters, has ordered ten more copies. He tells me that his immense bibliography, (his third so far!) The Librorum Prohibitorum, is progressing at some pace, with only around two hundred titles left to catalogue. It contains some rare jewels, including a first edition of that splendid magazine 'The Pearl,' which I published last year and that other minor classic, 'A Man With A Maid' Admittedly, they are of less literary value than your splendid translations, but they sell very well.

Have you read Swinburne's little book, 'The Whippingham Papers? I have just brought this out with a fine, leather tooled binding and I must say it has gone down rather well.

Yes, I should much appreciate it if you dropped in to see me at the Libertarian Bookshop. I have some fine hashish which needs smoking and we can make plans for your 'Scented Garden.'

Yours Ever, Leonard.

DOCTOR WATSON'S JOURNAL

My companion failed to appear at breakfast the following morning. Finding myself alone save for the excellent Mrs Hudson, I decided to read the morning edition of The Times. My attention was drawn to three articles. The first of these gave an account of the murder of Leonard Smith, giving a brief description of the circumstances and of his reputation as a publisher of erotica. The second piece, relegated to page two, gave a brief account of the mysterious disappearance of Mrs Beryl Baskerville of Baskerville Manor, concluding with the words: 'It is believed that Chief Inspector Lestrade from Scotland Yard is to investigate the matter.' There was no mention of my companion, which did not surprise me in the least. Holmes was never one to court publicity.

The third article was a review of a music hall at the New Lyceum, which had just re-opened under new management.

'For someone who enjoys the comic and the bizarre,' wrote the author of this short piece, 'one could do no better than to visit The New Lyceum which has recently been restored and is under new management. Last evening when I visited the theatre, I was entertained by several sharp comedians, and an escapologist by the name of Houdina - a female performer who enacted the famous American's water tank trick.'

I spent the remainder of the day in an aimless mood. By early evening Holmes still hadn't appeared so I decided to make my way along The Strand and, after a light dinner at Mancini's, arrived at the New Lyceum theatre.

The theatre had been well restored, its boxes with their cherub carvings carefully rendered, the ceiling painted with a large mural depicting The Rape of Lucrece, rather in the style of Rubens. The theatre was packed to the brim with a variety of clientele and food and strong drink was freely available. Indeed some people in the front rows seemed the worse for wear. We were first introduced by a flautist and dancing bear, a rather poignant business which produced much laughter among some sections of the audience. There followed a comedian with a Yorkshire accent who I found distinctly unfunny, some acrobats and a female singer who was slightly flat but who made up for her lame performance by revealing to us her ample bosom.

Then we came to the female escapologist. This proved to be an act equal in expertise to the original version, indeed it was made even more enjoyable by virtue of the artiste's brief costume which revealed her curvaceous figure and luxurious head of black hair. She possessed that olive skin which I have seen among certain Italian women. I have had, as I think I have often mentioned to Holmes, an experience of women spanning three continents and have had several encounters with ladies in north India which I fondly recall, and I regard myself as quite an arbiter of taste in such matters.

The performance came to a conclusion around ten thirty after a fire eater and a shabby genteel magician. Finding myself at something of a loose end, I decided I would make my way round to the artiste's dressing room to offer my congratulations to Beatrice, the escapologist. However, I found myself much disappointed, since she had already left. Clustered around the back door of the theatre was a collection of young women, some who I recognised from the troupe of can can dancers. One in particular caught my eye, a trim, blonde haired girl called Rachael, who approached me somewhat boldly and asked me if I should like to stroll with her down the Strand. Since it was a dry, starry night and not especially cold I complied with her suggestion. It soon proved, that despite my advancing years, we seemed to have much in common with each other and, by the time we had reached The Aldwych Hotel, it seemed in order that we should both drop in for a nightcap before my return to Baker Street. I found myself enchanted and fascinated by my young companion, who I found to be both intelligent and vivacious and, on parting at Charing Cross, we both resolved to meet the following evening after her work had concluded. Since I had been without a wife for some considerable length of time I deemed this to be entirely proper.

I returned to Baker Street at around eleven thirty to find Holmes still up. He looked pale and wan. He was stretched out on the basket chair wearing his blue smoking jacket and smoking his long cherrywood, which he often did when in a disputatious mood.

'You have been working late on a case?' I enquired.
'How very observant of you.'
'I try to emulate your methods, although I confess I do not always succeed.'
'Your honesty commends you. Now do allow me to continue in the same vein, my dear fellow.'
'Go ahead.'
'She is a blonde, young, with expensive tastes and she works as a dancer in the music hall. You find yourself attracted to her and intend to continue the relationship.'
I stared at him with a mixture of astonishment and embarrassment.
'How on earth…?'
'It really is quite simple. You return late in the evening, which is something that you rarely do. Your clothes carry a strong odour of tobacco and alcohol which indicates to me that you have spent some while in licensed premises. There is on your left coat lapel a long blonde hair. There is a third

odour which suggests to me lavender - a perfume of some quality and therefore likely to be expensive. There is also a trace of red lipstick on your shirt collar. Since you are most definitely a full blooded male and your wife is deceased, all of these factors would suggest a female encounter.'
'And the dancer in the music hall?'
'The ticket for the music hall. It is protruding from your top pocket. The words 'New Lyceum' are clearly visible. The Lyceum employs a number of young women as can can dancers. I confess that the last observation was somewhat conjectural.'
'You are right in every respect. Her name is Rachael. She is…'
'No need to give me the details. Your private life is entirely your own.'
'Very well. Then may I ask you how you spent your day?'
'Certainly. I have spent the majority of my day reading pornography.'
I raised my eyebrows at this admission.
'You may or may not be aware that such material is in much demand.'
'I am aware of that.'
'Let me elucidate. This morning, shortly after nine, I took a cab to Parker Street, just off The Kingsway.'
'To visit Smith's bookshop?'
'Yes, Watson, and I do not mean W H Smith's. At the bookshop I met the manager, a young, neurasthenic fellow with long flaxen hair, the business partner, who was eager to show me some of his more lurid stock of photographs and written material. I discovered some interesting facts about Leonard Smith. He had several patrons for whom he

supplied his material. The subscribers of his 'Erotikon Book Club' include Sir Richard Burton, the explorer, Oscar Wilde, and two members of our Royal Family, one of them being 'AV' who, you may recall, was involved in the Telegraph Boy Scandal.'

'Although the latter's presence at the brothel was never actually proved,' I observed.

'Admittedly,' Holmes agreed. 'Nevertheless, it seems that our victim had much support from members of High Society. Two other names on the list caught my attention.'

'Oh, and who might they be?'

'A leading cabinet member who, according to my brother Mycroft, must not be named, and a certain Henry Spencer Ashbee. Ashbee is a wealthy business man who was an associate of Smith. According to some correspondence I unearthed while I was rummaging around in the bookshop's back office - I had employed Wiggins to throw a stone through the shop window, serving as a distraction - Ashbee was closely involved in the resourcing and financing of Smith's pornographic empire. He is compiling a bibliography he calls 'The Index Librorum Prohibitorum' which lists the first editions of rare erotic works - some from the Roman period, which he has translated.'

'And you think this man Ashbee might be involved with Smith's murder?'

'I do not theorise without evidence, Watson, you of all people should know that! However, there is no doubt in my mind that the Erotikon Book Club and its illustrious members, because of their insatiable appetite, are highly vulnerable to blackmail.'

'You intend interviewing them?'

'I shall expect Lestrade to take care of that matter. Besides, I shall be busy with this Baskerville business.'
'No news yet regarding Beryl Baskerville?'
'Unfortunately not. And no clues yet as to the reason for her sudden disappearance. It is possible I shall have to go down to Dartmoor, which I am reluctant to do. Anyway, I expect Charles Mortimer to be calling on us tomorrow around two o'clock. Will you be here or will you be entertaining your lady friend?'
'I shall be here.'
'Oh, I forgot to mention - we shall soon be receiving another visitor to our hallowed rooms.'
'And who is that?'
'Dr Hans Gross. You may have heard of him?'
'I confess I have not.'
'Dr Gross is an Austrian magistrate and one of the world's most distinguished criminologists. He is also the author of two important works: 'Criminal Investigation' and 'Criminal Psychology.' You might like to read them, Watson, though I must warn you that both volumes are in the original German.'
'I have some grasp of the Teutonic tongue,' I replied, though my knowledge of German was admittedly rudimentary.
'Excellent. Here you are then,' and on saying, he reached up to the bookcase and brought down two heavy, leather bound books. Then he returned to the fireside where he proceeded to poke the dying embers and lit his cherrywood. I retired to bed where my mind wrestled with the complexities of the German language, but eventually

this fruitless task gave way to fond memories of my new *amour,* the delightful Rachael.

The following morning dawned bright with a cloudless sky. I slept late, my slumbers only disturbed by the loud rattle of a brewer's dray as it made its way through Upper Baker Street. I bathed and changed my shirt, conscious of the pervasive odour of lavender which still clung to my shirt collar. I thought of Rachael and felt deeply aroused in a way that I had not experienced since the death of my beloved wife Mary.

I found Holmes in a smoke - filled lounge. He was sitting in the basket chair, his eyes closed, his hawk like features etched in silhouette by the flames of the fire. As I took my usual place at the breakfast table, and, exuding a great billow of smoke, he looked directly at me.

'So what did you make of Gross's work?' he asked.
'Fascinating.'
'And the section on malingering?'
'Particularly helpful.'
'The use of eserine by beggars to contract the irises of their eyes is something I had noted in the case of Neville St Clair.'
'The Blackheath beggar?'
'Quite so. And what else impressed you?'

I was about to make a lame reply to the question when there was the sound of voices on the stair. Holmes sprang from his feet and, knocking the bowl of his pipe on the mantle, went to open the door.

'Who is it, Mrs Hudson?'
'Inspector Lestrade, Mr Holmes. He'd like a word with you.'
'By all means, show him up. You've no objection, Watson?'
'None whatsoever,' I replied incoherently, my mouth full of kipper.

Lestrade looked even wearier than when I had last seen him. His shiny black pomaded hair was tousled, there were bags under his eyes and there was a strong smell of sweat.

'What news, Lestrade?'
'None that's good, Mr Holmes, I'm sorry to report to you that our friend the garrotter…'
'Parker is dead.'
'How did you know about it? The news hasn't yet been released to the Press.'
'I have my informants.'
'You are correct. His body turned up in The Thames last night. One of the wherrymen found him just under Vauxhall Bridge. I must say that you don't seem surprised at this.'
'It is what I would have expected. I could have predicted it.'
'How so?'

'Because the fate of Parker bears all the hallmarks of the Moriarty gang.'
'But Professor Moriarty died at the Reichenbach Falls,' I pointed out.
Holmes' face darkened.
'Moriarty may have died, Watson, but his legacy of organised crime has not. In fact, if anything, it has grown since his disappearance.'
'You don't think that he may still be alive?' I asked.
'We can only conjecture. And though his henchman, Colonel Sebastian Moran, was imprisoned for his crimes and paid the price for his iniquities, there are many other gang members still operating Moriarty's empire - an organisation based on fear and depravity. What was the cause of death, Inspector?'
'He had been strangled.'
'From behind?'
'Garrotted. So the police surgeon tells me.'
Holmes nodded.
'A favourite method of execution by the Moriarty gang. A slow, lingering death, since the garrotte is tightened by small increments. I have known them use a golf ball, which fits inside the garrotting cloth, and gradually crushes the victim's windpipe.'
'It seems that this fellow Parker had a number of other strings to his bow,' observed Lestrade. 'He and another fellow, John Wymondham, ran a number of brothels around Paddington Station and Charing Cross. Several of these establishments specialised in what they describe as 'correction services.' Last week a team of my officers raided one of these establishments just off the Charing

Cross Road. The ground floor of the premises was operating as what the owner, a Cypriot, described to us as 'an erotic bookshop.' The two upper floors housed the bawdy house. When we raided the place we found a series of rooms devoted to punishment and domination. We seized a horde of flagellation equipment. In the largest of the rooms we found a fully operating medieval type rack, complete with its rollers and ratchet mechanisms. There was a fellow there on the rack, entirely naked. When interrogated, he turned out to be a member of the King's Household Cavalry. He had the cheek to offer one of my officers the princely sum of a hundred pounds to keep his name out of The Press! The establishment was staffed with ten girls - I call them girls because the oldest must have been no more than nineteen, the youngest probably as young as twelve.'

'These girls - what nationality were they?' Holmes enquired, thoughtfully.

'Mixed. Some were Indian, a few from South America, I should say, and there were a couple of French and Italians.'

'Supplied, no doubt, by the international sex slave trade. This is most interesting. Thank you, Lestrade. Your information is invaluable.'

'Pleased to be of service, Mr Holmes.'

'I also have been some investigating. According to one of my informants, Parker was also the proprietor of two opium dens in Upper Swandam Lane, near to the docks in Rotherhithe. I visited one of the establishments last evening and found that it was in the hands of a Lascar whose face was familiar to me from the Blackheath mendicant business. You recall it, Watson?'

'We were reminiscing about it only this morning.'

'Just so. Your friend Isa Whitney was a regular customer there. How are Kate and Isa, by the way?'

'Kate died of consumption about a year ago. Since then, Isa has fallen into something of a decline.'

'Opium?'

'I'm afraid so.'

'Watson here would have it that my weekly appointment with Morpheus is affecting my faculties, Lestrade. Frankly, I am reluctant to believe it. Anyway, I digress. Whilst I was at Swandam Lane, in the guise of a myopic, elderly academic, I got into conversation with one of the den's regular users. He told me that two men often visited there, one answering Parker's description, the other, a taller, much thinner man with short, dark hair. The latter was always well dressed, wore a pair of black gloves and spoke with a refined accent. Every Friday, both men would disappear into one of the back rooms, then emerge about half an hour later, carrying cloth bags which he assumed were the weekly takings. From what I could deduce, the packaged opium was brought up the river by a wherry to the rear of the premises where it was hoisted up to the first floor by these two Lascars. I am of the opinion that there is a deal more to learn about these two, but I shall be hard pressed to make a connection with the Moriarty gang.'

'I have every confidence that you will succeed, Mr Holmes,' said Lestrade.

'We cannot assume that. The Moriarty organisation is much like the Hydra. No sooner have you cut off one head, then another grows in its place. Nevertheless…'

There was a sudden sound of breaking glass. The next thing I knew, Holmes had reeled backwards, landing on the fireplace rug. I turned to glance at the window which had partly shattered and cracked from the impact of a bullet. Lestrade rushed over to the window and surveyed the houses opposite, whilst I administered first aid.

'It is nothing, Watson, a mere scratch,' he protested, struggling to stand up.
'Let me at least clean the wound and bandage it.'
'Very well. Did you see anyone?' he asked Lestrade.
'I can see no one, save a solitary road sweeper. I thought that we had done with this kind of thing, Mr Holmes.'
'Clearly a wrong assumption.'
His arm now in an improvised sling, Holmes peered at the wall behind the sideboard, then took a penknife from his waistcoat pocket.
'Ah, here it is. Let me see…this bullet is from a Martini-Henry rifle, optimum range about six hundred yards. Much like the Enfield but more accurate. You will recall they were much in use during the Afghan wars, Watson. It has been fired from a first floor window from the house opposite.'
'Indeed. More to the point, who is trying to assassinate you?' I asked.

Chapter Four

INTERRUPTION

Letter from Aubrey Beardsley to Leonard Smith: October 1st, 1897, Cosmopolitan Hotel, Manton, France.

Dear Leonard,

Thank you for the proofs of the play Lysistrata, which I received this morning. I am sorry to inform you that I no longer wish to represent my drawings in any future editions of this work, nor indeed any of the other so-called erotic pictures which I have supplied to your publications over the past decade.

As you may know, I have been suffering from the effects of this wretched condition. Here in Manton the air is fresher, the climate more agreeable and the streets far less polluted than those of London. It is a medieval town, and the Basilique Saint Michel is a wonder to behold. So here I shall remain, at least while I can afford it. The doctor told me I must at all costs avoid stress and a damp climate. Manton is a most beautiful town. Here, on the riviera, we enjoy many sunny days and in winter it is not nearly so cold as it can be in England. My doctor tells me my lungs are quite shot through and that I should at most enjoy another year before entering the shadow lands. I am, as you can plainly see, a poor wretch. When I am gone - I have made a will and you will certainly receive some of my unpublished drawings for the friendship and encouragement you have shown me over the years - I hope that I may be remembered for my contribution to the world of art.

I have recently undergone a change in my direction and beliefs. It was whilst on one of my many visits to the Basilique that I experienced an epiphany. There is something about the rendering of God's word in Latin which gives the Testament an added authority and since becoming a Catholic I have understood the importance of confession. And I have much to confess, not least my sinful relationship with my sister Mabel, a matter which still continues to haunt me.

I hear that you have great ambitions for future publications in collaboration with this fellow Henry Ashbee. I once visited him at his house at the invitation of his son, who was one of our kind. His collection, which is vast and eclectic, occupies the top floor of the house. When I was last there in '85, he told me about an autobiography he was editing, by an author called Walter, who claimed to have enjoyed intercourse with thousands of women. I cannot believe this to be true. And truth is a most precious quality, which is at the root of all my best work. Which brings me back to the point I began with. I urge you to destroy all copies of my work which are bad or obscene, so that I can rest easy with my conscience. It is too late to stop the Lysistra edition and for that you are forgiven.

Yours ever,

Aubrey.

PS: Have you heard anything from dear Oscar? I have received no communication from when he moved to France.

Letter from Leonard Smith to Aubrey Beardsley, October 12th, 1897

My Dear Aubrey,

I was sorry to learn of your declining condition. We knew that you had had a previous encounter with this cursed illness some years back but hoped that you might have banished it.

I will admit that I was somewhat disappointed about your reluctance to continue publishing your fine illustrations. I still have the set of drawings you completed for the limited edition of The Priapeia Index, a fine book which was one of our earliest successes. Would you like me to send you these? I could also include the five volume edition of 'Walter', which Ashbee has now completed. It is an astounding collection of reminiscences which pushes the reader to the utmost limits of human sexuality and I urge you to read it, for it is a work of unvarnished truth, though too hot for any conventional publisher to handle. By virtue of your continued membership of the Erotikon Club, you are entitled to free copies of the work.

You enquire about Oscar. He is living with Ross in Berneval le Grand, Northern France. Ross has been kind to him and has done much to heal his wounds, poor fellow. His plight has been much of his own making, but he does not see it. He asked The Society of Jesus to grant him a six month retreat but sadly they refused him. He has become something of a martyr and now goes under the name of 'Sebastian Melmoth,' named partly after Saint Sebastian, shot to death with arrows, and Melmoth The Wanderer, the book written by his uncle, Charles Maturin.

What a pity he could not continue to satisfy his desires without recourse to legal process. We all subscribed to a first class arrangement regarding the London hotels, the bell boys and telegraph boys which might have happily continued, were it not for Oscar's arrest and subsequent confinement. Thankfully, the organisation to which we paid our subscriptions still continues to provide an excellent service and the quality of the boys supplied to us is without reproach.

But I must not blame the poor fellow. He has suffered much. Let us hope Ross will revive his spirits. I hear that he, like you, intends joining the Roman Church. I fear that for my own part, I am bound for the inferno!

Yours,

Leonard.

Letter from Oscar Wilde to Leonard Smith, July 1899, L'Hotel, Rue des Beaux Arts, St Germaine des Pres, Paris

My Dear Leonard,

Your letter and its enclosures came to me as a most pleasant surprise. Of late my spirits have been somewhat low and I feel that those who once supported me have deserted me utterly. Even dear Robbie has not visited me ever since his family threatened to dispossess him. I find myself living in a state of abject poverty here in this grubby section of the city. The hotel is filthy, my rooms dark and dank and I find myself eking out a meagre existence supported only by the few pounds a week supplied by Constance. I cannot even see my son, such is the opprobrium that has been levelled against me. Without the support of my wife, I am lost. She was with me throughout the troubled times, but she has grown weary of my peccadilloes. What little money I have left after my hotel bill is paid, I spend on strong drink.

The volume you kindly sent to me by this man Walter intrigues me. I wonder who Walter really is. Can it be Ashbee, the erotic bibliophile? I am half persuaded that it is he that has penned these remarkably honest memoirs. What extraordinary stamina the fellow has! It seems that he started his amorous activities having been seduced when very young, and then continued without a break for several decades! At times I am persuaded that the author is a complete fantasist, for surely no sane person would undertake such a quest. Yet there is a strong feeling that it is the unvarnished, naked truth. It is also true that it is not a literary work; the language is crude, the style ungainly and the plot nothing more than a vulgar picaresque. If it were ever published by one of the principal London publishers, it would attract poor reviews - all of which persuades me that it is not by Ashbee after all, for he has a modicum of style.

What other treasures have you and Ashbee conjured up since my cruel confinement? I am eager to see more. Much of this sort of material available to me in Paris is cheap stuff and poorly produced, often printed on cheap paper. There is nothing in this great city like the work you produce for our book club, with those elegant bindings and gilt edged, leather covers.

There is also nothing here to compare with what was on offer to us in London. There are boys to hire here, but in the main they are but ragged street urchins, many of them little more than desiccated skeletons. I am often filled with nostalgia for those gaudy nights we spent together in the West End and at the Cadogan Hotel, though those memories are also still a constant source of pain to me. I hope that if I ever return to London - perhaps in the after life - I might resume my association with that excellent group of young men supplied by your fine organisation.

I live in hope.

Yours,

Melmoth.

DOCTOR WATSON'S DIARY

Shortly after three o'clock, there was a sound of rattling wheels from the street and shortly afterwards Mrs Hudson announced our visitor. My companion, who, following Lestrade's departure, had downed a brandy and fallen asleep by the fireside, suddenly woke and leapt to his feet. His eyes glistening, he resembled a falcon who had just caught the scent of his prey.

'Dr Mortimer, welcome. I see you have been delayed,' said Holmes. 'Pray, come and warm yourself by the fire. A pot of tea for our visitor, Mrs Hudson.'
'Very well, Mr Holmes.'
I took Dr Mortimer's coat and he settled into one of the basket chairs.
'You have been injured, I see,' observed Mortimer.
'It is nothing serious, just a flesh wound.'
'Nevertheless, you should let me examine you.'
'That will not be necessary. Watson here has already administered first aid.'
'Forgive me Dr Watson. I should have remembered.'

'You are forgiven. We have not set eyes on each other for the last twelve years.'

'It has been a considerable interval,' observed Holmes. 'Tell me, how is Sir Henry dealing with the crisis?'

'Quite badly, I'm afraid. That is partly why I have come to see you today. Sir Henry is a troubled man.'

'For how long has this been the case?'

'For these past ten years.'

'Was he not happily married?'

'Oh yes, entirely happy. They were, as far as I am concerned, deeply in love. And still are, I am sure.'

'Children?'

'Sadly not. There was a boy, born five years ago, but he died, aged only three months.'

'But this is not the cause of his current indisposition?'

'No. Let me elucidate.'

'Pray do. And please, stick to the facts.'

Holmes reached for his oldest black brier and lit it, enveloping us all in a cloud of dense gray smoke.

'Ever since the conclusion of this business of Stapleton, Sir Henry has become more and more obsessed with legend of the hound.'

'In what way?'

'Despite the evidence which you and I presented to him, he remains convinced that there is truth in the legend of the family curse.'

'But that is quite irrational.'

'Maybe so, but that is what he truly believes. It has become what the French psychologists describe as 'an idee fixe.'

'You mean a monomania?'

'No Watson, that is subtly different,' said Holmes. 'A monomania is a state of madness, or derangement of the mind. The *idée fixe* is a single pathology of the intellect. The '*idée fixe*' may be trifling in character, and accompanied by complete sanity in every other way. A man might form such an *idée fixe* and under its influence be capable of any fantastic outrage.'
'Well defined, Mr Holmes.'
'Please continue.'
'He has spent many years researching the legends concerning black dogs and the hell hound. He has discovered that the body of Sir Hugo, his notorious ancestor, was interred in a tomb in the graveyard of Buckfastleigh Church. I have visited the place myself and it possesses an eerie presence.'
'Much like the moor itself.'
'Quite so, Dr Watson.'
'I found my brief residence on the moor quite agreeable,' said Holmes, 'and not all eerie. It has an atmosphere and identity which is unique. But please do continue, doctor.'
'Last year he discovered, quite by accident, that he was indirectly related on his mother's side of the family, to another notorious ancestor, one Richard Cabell. The Cabell family come from the East of England - Cromer, in Norfolk, to be precise.'
'Watson and I know the place well. We visited the town when we investigated the curious case of The Dancing Men.'
'Well, this Cabell character murdered his wife some time in the 1600's. Thereafter he was haunted by a large phantom dog, known locally as Old Shuck. Old Shuck is

the grimmest apparition of the Norfolk coast. He takes the form of a huge black dog with a single flashing eye and a mouth that breathes forth fire, and to encounter him is an omen of dread significance: it means that you will die before the year is out. It is, perhaps, the oldest phantom in England; it has haunted our lonely roads for centuries. Probably it is of Norse origin - the Black Hound of Odin - and came to this coast with the Scandinavian raiders. Its lair is some secret place known only to itself, but some of its favourite haunts are known, and not many years ago there were men and women who nothing would induce to venture into them after nightfall. When the wind howled around their isolated homes, it was the baying of Old Shuck they heard, and they trembled in their beds.'

'Yes, yes,' remonstrated Holmes, 'this is all very well, Mortimer, but what of the facts?'

'The facts are these. This obsession of Sir Henry has grown quite out of proportion, so that, since his return from East Anglia he has become a virtual recluse and rarely leaves his study where he has made a virtual prisoner of himself, despite the protestations of Beryl, who does her best to humour him. He has also developed the insane notion that he is the victim of lycanthropy.'

Holmes leaned forwards at this point, his hands steepled. 'Explain.'

'Very well, I shall. Last winter Sir Henry visited Cromer where he spent several days looking into the local legend of the Black Dog. The home of the Cabells lies to the north of the town and the Cabell family are, even to this day, benefactors to the local inhabitants. He spent some time talking to the present owner of Cabell House, which is a

large gothic mansion, set in its own parkland. It was there that Sir Robert Cabell told Sir Henry of the origin of their family curse - a curse which implies that a tragic and unnatural death will befall all of the male offspring of the family.'
'And the origin of the curse? What of that?'
Doctor Mortimer picked up a small leather attache case and drew from it a large scroll of parchment.
'Before Sir Henry left for the West Country, he was given a copy of this Cabell family document. May I read it to you?'
'Yes, if it has a direct bearing on the matter.'
It does. The document is dated 1686. It reads as follows:

'A true Discourse (the document read) Declaring the Damnable life and death of one Lord Richard Cabell, A most wicked sorcerer, who, in the likeness of a wolf, committed many murders, killing and devouring many women and children. Who, for the same fact was taken and executed on the 31st October 1547 in the Towne of Cromer.

'Those whome the Lord doth leaue to followe the Imagination of their owne hartes, dispising his proffered grace, in the end through the hardnes of hart and contempt of his fatherly mercy, they enter the right path of perdicion and destruction of the body and sole for euer.

'Such a one was the bloody and murderous Lord Cabell who, from his youth, was greatly inclined to euil and the practising of wicked Artes euen from twelue yeers of age till twentye, and so forwards till his dying day. The Deuill, who hath a readye ear to listen to the lewde motions of cursed men, promised to give vnto him whatsoeuer his hart desired during his mortall life: whereupon this vile wretch desired great riches and that at his pressure he might work his lust and malice on men, women and children, in the shape of a beast. So the Deuill who sawe in him a fit instrument to perfourm mischeefe as a wicked feend, gaue unto him a girdle which, being put about him, he was transfourmed into the likeness of a greedy deuouring Woolf, strong and mighty, with eyes great and large, which in the night sparkeled like vnto brandes of fire, a mouth great and wide, with most sharp and cruell teeth. A huge body and mighty pawes.

'Lord Cabell was heerwith exceedingly pleased. And he grew rich by the transforming of base metal into gold, being known to all and sundrey as a most respectable citizen, whilst at night in Woolfish likeness, he would indulge his filthy luste, walking abroad in the fields and laying holde of maidens and children alike: and after his luste was fulfilled, he would murder them presentlye. Thus within the compass of a few yeeres he had murdered thirteene yong children and two yong women bigge with Child, tearing the children out of their wombes in most bloody and sauage sorte and after eate their hearts panting hotte and rawe, which he accounted dainty morsels & best agreeing to his Appetite.

'Thus this damnable Lord Cabell liued the tearme of fiue and twenty yeeres, unsuspected to be Author of so many cruell and vnaturall murders, in which time he had destroyed and spoyled an vnknown number of Men, Women and Children, sheepe, lambes and goates. And although they had practised all the meanes that men could deuise to take this rauenous beast, yet until the Lord had determined his fall, the inhabitants of Cromer could not in any wise preuaille: notwithstanding they daylye continued their purpose, and dayly sought to entrap him, and for that intent continually maintained great mastyes and Dogges of much strength to hunt and chase the beast wheresoeer they could finde him.

' At length it pleased God that they shoulde find him in a field, tearing the vitals from a sheep and presently he slipped his girdle from him whereby the shape of a Woolfe cleaune auoided, and he appeared presently in his true shape & likeness: this wrought a wonderfull amazement in their mindes and they came unto him and talking with him they brought him home to his owne house and finding him to be the man indeede, they had him incontinent before the Maiestrates to be examined.

'Thus being apprehended, he was shortly after put to the racke in the City of Norwich, but fearing torture he voluntarily confessed his whole life and made known the villanies which he had committed for the space of xxv yeares.

'After he had some space beene imprisoned, the maiestrates found him guilty of these abominable acts and Lord Cabell was iudged first to have his body laide on a wheel, and with red hotte pincers in ten seueral places to haue the flesh puld off from the bones, after that, his legges and Arms to be broken with a wooden Axe or Hatchet, afterwards his head strook from his body, then to haue his carcase burnde to Ashes.

'Thus Gentle Reeder haue I set down the true discourse of this wicked man Lord Gresham, which I desire to be a warning to all Sorcerers and Witches which unlawfully followe their own diuellish imagination to the utter ruine and destruction of their soules eternally. Amen.'

Dr Mortimer finished reading, and took off his spectacles.
'What do you make of it, Mr Holmes?'
'As I think I may have observed before, it is of interest only to a collector of fairy tales.'
'Then how would you account for the fact that Sir Henry has become a creature of nocturnal habits?'
'He does not sleep well?'
'He sleeps for much of the day and twice I have found him at one of the upstairs rooms, staring at the moon.'
'You believe he is fulfilling his deepest fears?'
'I believe he may be a lycanthrope. It is an unusual condition.'
'You may be right. Notions that lycanthropy was due to a medical condition go back to the second century, when the Alexandrian physician Paulus Aegineta attributed

lycanthropy to melancholy or an excess of black bile. In fact we know now that it is a delusion.'

'Could his condition have affected his relationship with Beryl?' I asked.

'Quite possibly, doctor.'

'But it does not explain her disappearance. Watson, hand me the Bradshaw, will you? Thank you. Ah, I see there is a fast train leaving Paddington at three thirty.'

'You will take on the case then?' asked Mortimer.

'There is little choice in the matter. I believe there is more to this affair than meets the eye, Watson. On the surface, it appears to be quite elementary, and yet…these are deep waters, and who knows what dark terrain they will lead us to?'

Chapter Five

DR WATSON'S JOURNAL

It was not long before Holmes, Dr Mortimer and I were sitting snugly inside a first-class railway carriage at Paddington Station, footwarmers tucked beneath our tartan blankets, watching the endless rows of freshly built suburban streets stretch away on either side of us.

"See, doctor, the drones have not been idle," Holmes remarked, whose loathing for the provincial architecture of his own age was profound. I said nothing in reply but sank back into my seat and observed the blotched terrain of suburban London give way to the rolling hills of Dorset and Devon. Here and there the skyline would be broken by a cluster of thatched cottages, each with its own distinctly Norman church. But my thoughts were far away at this point and specifically orientated to matters of the female form to notice details.

As dusk slowly fell and Holmes began to invade the carriage with his acrid pipe smoke we passed into an altogether lonelier terrain of the moor itself where there were few hedgerows and even fewer hamlets to break up the monotony of the journey. There was a great eeriness and loneliness about this countryside as I watched it slipping into the darkness. It was like a face on which all the creases had been removed and you were left staring at a ancient, undulating skin.

The train drew in to a succession of small stations, then lurched once more upon its way. I was struck by the lack of human figures in the landscape. Only once was the pattern broken when we drew level to a small group of travellers on the road, which lay parallel to the track. The driver of the fly was a man probably in his mid-twenties, yet the harshness of his existence had lined his face and drawn crows' feet around his eyes. His wife and child sat huddled in the back of the vehicle, their eyes dull and tinged with melancholy. After such a sight I began to hanker after the gaudy London streets which I had known from childhood.

At last the train juddered to a halt and we emerged amid a cloud of acrid steam onto the platform at Bovey Tracey. Fortunately a cob and four wheeler had been provided for our convenience by Sir Henry's butler and we were whisked out of the ancient town and onto a series of rough, uneven roads where clusters of twisted oak trees predominated. Eventually we passed over a low bridge and down a narrow dirt track. There ahead of us stood the tall, imposing towers of Baskerville Hall, outlined against the darkening sky.

As I got out of the four wheeler, the sun, which had followed us from Bristol, sank behind a bank of inky-black cloud. Already the distant hills had turned to a dirty dun colour. Although I had been here before and remembered it only too well, the building before me seemed unreal as if a giant hand had placed it there. The spiralling towers and narrow, shuttered windows gave expression to its pale walls and ivy-covered gateway. A dull light shone through heavy mullioned windows, and from the high chimneys which rose from the steep, high-angled roof, there sprang a column of black smoke.

We entered the hallway and Barrymore took our bags from the fly. A door to our left opened and Sir Henry Baskerville emerged to greet us. He looked drawn and thinner than when I had last seen him twelve years ago, and he had grown a bushy black beard. There were deep lines to his brow and he seemed weary.

'Gentlemen, I am relieved to see you once more. You are welcome, Mr Holmes, Doctor. Some refreshment perhaps?'
He looked across at Barrymore who nodded and left the room.
'Come into the lounge where we can chat before dinner is served.'

He rang a bell and, as we settled into comfortable chairs beside a roaring fire, a maid soon appeared at the door.
'Sophie, the drinks tray for our visitors.'

Sophie, a tall, buxom, rosy cheeked girl in her late teens, curtseyed, then left the room, returning almost immediately with a well stocked tray. As she leaned over to pour my whisky, I became aware of a strong smell of some musk - based perfume which I found somewhat arousing and the face of Rachael floated before me.

After a generous meal of roast beef and treacle pudding, accompanied by one of Sir Henry's rich Tokay wines, we retired to the study where we sat for a while and smoked cigars. Then Holmes lit his favourite brier and, turning to Sir Henry, said quietly:

'Now that we have some privacy, may I ask you some questions regarding your wife's disappearance, Sir Henry?'

'Happy to tell you what I know, Mr Holmes. Shoot,' he replied in his rich Canadian accent.

'About your relationship with Beryl. Would you describe it as good, satisfactory, or problematic?'

'My, that's a blunt question!'

'As you may know, I am not prone to circumlocution. A straight answer if you please.'

'Satisfactory then. No marriage is without its difficulties as I am sure you appreciate.'

'Quite so, although personally, I have had no experience of marriage.'

'Beryl is, as you may recall, and as Dr Mortimer will confirm, a very passionate and fiery woman who has suffered greatly from the hands of that beast, Stapleton. The strong attachment we have developed often leads to conflict.'

'You have had many rows?'

'Quite a number over the past few years. I don't mind admitting it. Beryl is a headstrong woman, who likes to get her own way. She would have made a splendid suffragette!'

Dr Mortimer laughed at this suggestion, but Holmes remained serious.

'Was there any matter in particular which led to these differences of opinion?'

'There were two topics in particular which led to our *contre tempes*. As Dr Mortimer may have told you, four years ago, we were blessed with a child, a boy who we named Michael. Sadly, he did not live long.'

Sir Henry's face darkened with emotion.

'The poor child died of an unidentified toxin,' added Dr Mortimer.

'Was there an inquest?'

'It was not considered necessary. Besides, my wife has strong views about the sanctity of the body. Anyway, after tragedy struck us, Beryl fell into a deep depression.'

'What was the other flash point?' asked Holmes, brusquely.

'As I believe Dr Mortimer has told you, recently - about a year ago now - I started doing some research into my family's origins and ancestry.'

Holmes nodded.

'Go on.'

'I discovered, purely by chance, that my mother's family were related to the Cabell family, whose seat is in Norfolk. I took the opportunity of visiting the old Manor House at Cromer where I met the present incumbent, Sir Robert Cabell. It was he who told me about the legend of the Black Dog and the curse…'

'And you believe you may also be affected by this curse?'

'I am certain of it.'

'Even though there is not a shred of evidence to prove that lycanthropy exists as a physical affliction?'
'Even so. I have noticed changes about myself.'
'Such as?'
'Small things. A terrible hunger for raw meat, an increase in body hair, and - I say this in the utmost confidence -' Here his voice lowered. 'I have had terrible, most vivid fantasies.'
'About what?'
'About women, Mr Holmes. And about the consummation of my imaginings. Violent, lustful imaginings, too terrible to describe in detail. Dr Mortimer and I visited the metropolis to see a Harley Street specialist, Sir Charles Banks. I told him of my feelings. He told me that I was suffering from something called 'satyriasis.'
'An increase of sexual desire, the male version of nymphomania,' I interjected.
'Thank you, Watson. Did he offer a remedy?' asked Holmes.
'Only that I should spend some time in one of the high class bawdy houses in the West End.'
Holmes suppressed a smile.
'And did you take his advice?'
'I confess I did. However, that has failed to quench my appetite.'
'You have told your wife about this?' I asked.
'I dare not. It is too dreadful to contemplate.'
'But you continue to enjoy conjugal relations with Beryl?'
'Not for some while now. She believes that I am in the grip of an obsession, but she refuses to discuss the matter with me. She spends much of her time wandering upon the

moors or working at the Women's Mission at Bovey Tracey.'

'The Women's Mission? What is that?' asked Holmes.

'It is a charitable organisation to assist the plight of fallen women,' explained Dr Mortimer. 'Beryl and Laura Lyons, old Frankland's daughter, founded the Mission five years ago. They have done much to assist some of these poor drabs who one sees daily wandering the streets of Princetown and Tavistock. They provide food, shelter and moral support.'

'They both suffered at the hands of that fellow Stapleton. I imagine that they have much in common,' I observed.

'Yes, they are very close friends. After that dreadful business of the Hound, Laura was much concerned about Beryl's mental state. As you know, she suffered a great deal of physical and emotional damage.'

'What does Laura make of Beryl's disappearance?'

'She believes that someone abducted her.'

'On what evidence does she base this opinion?' asked Holmes.

'The day before she disappeared, she met Laura in Bovey Tracey. Laura said Beryl seemed very distracted and had clearly been crying. She told her she had seen someone in the town - someone from her past. Laura pressed her on the matter but she refused to tell her who it was. I only wish she had confided in me, Mr Holmes, I really do. I blame myself for what has happened. My self obsession and self regard…'

'You must not proportion blame to yourself, Sir Henry. This is a more complex matter than it appears to be.'

'You think you may know where Beryl is?'

'At present I do not. However, there are certain features to this matter which I find interesting. At this stage of my investigation it would be imprudent of me to say more.'
Sir Henry glanced at his fob watch.
'It is late, gentlemen. I shall ring for Barrymore and he will show you to your rooms.'

Holmes, Barrymore and I made our way up the ornate staircase to our rooms. At the end of a broad landing a pointed window reflected the last rays of light of the setting sun. Elsewhere, the passageway lay swathed in muted browns and greys. I found that I could see through a transparent pane of glass at the head of the stair which gave me a panoramic view of the house and its surroundings. Past the courtyard, the view, illuminated by the powerful Edison lamps, swept into the vast expanse of wood and brush and then on to the high ridge, now concealing the sun. Thick ivy covered this side of the Hall and on either side lancet windows peered like tiny eyes over the shadowy gardens. I reached out and drew my hand over the coloured panes. Their touch was cold and unwelcoming. An heraldic sign, inlaid with thorns and briars, lay there, executed in preraphaelite fashion. The motif was one I had never seen before, a wolf's head mounted on a pole, the mouth bloody and gaping. Through the lower jaw a broad sword had been thrust upwards. The oddness of the design was reinforced by the creature's eyes, which seemed particularly human in intent. The colours were violent, the patterns intricate.

'Whose arms are these ?' Holmes asked.

'Some distant ancestor of the Baskervilles, I believe,' replied Barrymore.

'There is an inscription, a signature - look, Watson, right in the corner. I confess I had not noticed it before. I can just make out the letters: 'Cabell.'

At length, overcome by fatigue (for the journey had been a long and tedious one) I must have drifted off into a fitful doze for I recall dreaming of a wide lake adjoining a ruined castle whose encrusted battlements were lined with ravens. Their glassy eyes shone luminously above me as I waded into the cold waters. Trapped in a cataleptic trance, I felt the cold waters lapping over my face and filling my mouth until I began to choke for dear life. When I awoke, I found Holmes staring down at me with a sardonic grin.

'Shhh...Not a word. Follow me,' Holmes whispered. Following his instruction, I donned my dressing gown and we made our way silently down the dark corridor. At the end of the landing, Holmes paused. A dull light spilled from a bedroom door which lay half closed. Through the crack of the door, I witnessed a shocking sight. Sir Henry lay on the bed, his lower half entirely exposed. Above him stood the buxom figure of Sophie Richards, the maid. She too was unclothed, save for a pair of tight fitting, black lace camisoles. Her shining blonde tresses had been let down to her waist, cascading over her voluptuous back and ample breasts as she strode back and forth across the room, then approached her subject with a slight run. By the light of the guttering oil lamp, I watched as she wielded a long leather riding stock, bringing it down with some strength in swift, sharp blows upon Sir Henry's reddened buttocks.

Silently, we both turned from this shocking sight and made our way back to our respective bedrooms, Holmes instructing me to say not a word about the cruel sight we had just witnessed. For some while afterwards I lay in my bed, sleep evading me, scarcely believing what I had just witnessed. I am a man of the world and had known of this kind of occurrence during my army service whilst in Afghanistan, indeed, such self abuse was common among many of the public school educated officers, yet I had not thought Sir Henry to be capable of such a perversion. I began to wonder if this was the real reason why Beryl had disappeared. Perhaps she had unwittingly come across the pair and had been so shocked by this unnatural perversion that she had decided to become incognito. There was also the matter of Sir Henry's wild obsession with lycanthropy and his increasing sexual appetite which may also have been manifested to her. Perhaps she had been the subject of some violent assault by her husband and fled in the night to her womens' refuge. These thoughts and the awful scene we had both witnessed kept drifting into my consciousness. I saw, over and again, Sir Henry's flailed and reddened rear and his well muscled, semi-clothed assailant running from one end of the bedroom to the other like some wild dervish. Was his intention to quell his base instincts by this cruel method and had he paid the maid for this savage beating? Or was it but one more feature of his satyriasis and, if so, what other depraved acts had he committed?

I had intended to talk to Holmes about the matter the following morning, but I awoke late, feeling exhausted by our night's adventure. I dressed and shaved quickly and made my way down to the breakfast room where I found Holmes and Sir Henry. They had both finished eating and Holmes had lit his oily brier. I thought that Sir Henry looked pale and tired, which did not come as a surprise to me.

'Ah, there you are, Watson, and how did you sleep?'
Used to such pawkish humour, I nevertheless felt myself blush.
'I slept well,' I replied, helping myself to a bowl of porridge.
'I feel that I must apologise for the lack of staff this morning,' said Sir Henry. 'It happens to be Barrymore's day off and for some unaccountable reason our maid Sophie is missing from her post.'
'Is she usually unreliable?' asked Holmes.
'Certainly not. Sophie is a willing and biddable young woman who will always do as she is instructed. She had excellent credentials. Her previous employer was a university professor.' The irony of this remark almost made me smile.
'High praise indeed! Tell me, Sir Henry, how well did she get on with your wife?'
'Very well - mostly. There was, I admit, one altercation between them.'
'When was this?'
'Oh, about a week ago.'

'Do you know what this was about?'

'I have no idea and, besides, Beryl refused to tell me about it.'

'Did that not strike you as unusual?'

'Not really. We both lead quite independent lives, Mr Holmes. I would that it were otherwise, for I am of the old school which believes that women are the gentler sex and sometimes need protecting. Beryl, on the other hand is what the Press have described as a 'New Woman.' She likes to do things for herself. She has an unquenchable spirit, that's for sure.'

'You said yesterday that she fell into a deep depression after the death of your son, Michael. Has that affected your relations?'

'It has left us both with scars, Mr Holmes. The death of a child is not an easy thing to overcome, as you may imagine. I am the sort of guy who tends to bottle things up, but Beryl is quite the contrary.'

Holmes nodded thoughtfully as he relit his pipe. I was about to join in with the conversation when there was a knock on the door.

'Come!' Sir Henry shouted.

A short, stout woman with grey hair stood in the doorway, wiping her hands on her apron.

'It's the police, sir, come about Miss Sophie. A police inspector.'

'Very well, cook, send him in.'

A tall, dapper man with a plump, ruddy face soon appeared at the door to our breakfast, accompanied by another, younger man.

'Sir Henry?'

'That's me.'
'This is Detective Constable Clarke and I am Chief Inspector Merrivale. We're here to inform you about one of your staff, Sir Henry.'
'Sophie Richards - you've found her?'
'We have found her body on the Moor.'
When was this?'
'About an hour ago. By Stippledown Rocks.'
'The old quarry?'
'A walker found her. Apparently, she had fallen from one of the rocky outcrops.'
'An accident?'
'Difficult to say at this stage of our investigation.'
'I'm very distressed to hear of it.'
'Inspector, would you object if I examined the scene of this unfortunate event?' asked Holmes.
'Forgive me, inspector. This is Mr Holmes and this is Dr Watson,' Sir Henry explained. 'They are my guests and will be staying with us for a few days regarding the disappearance of my wife, Beryl.'
'I thought I recognised you, Mr Holmes. I'd be honoured for you to join us. Didn't you assist Inspector Lestrade of the Yard regarding that business of the hound?'
'Indeed I did, though Lestrade must take the full credit for that case,' said Holmes, rising to greet the inspector. 'Tell me, has the place where you found Miss Richards been preserved?'

Inspector Merrivale nodded. 'As far as is possible considering the state of the weather. It rained quite a deal in the night and the ground was quite muddy. We found a couple of clear prints.'

'A man or a woman's?'
'I can't be certain. One was larger than the other, though.'
'Did you manage to preserve the prints?'
'We did, using your plaster of Paris method.'
Holmes smiled.
'You have read my monograph on the tracing of footprints then?'
'Indeed I have, sir. It is a standard text among our detective force here in Devonshire.'
'And how many of your men attended the body?'
'Just myself and a constable - oh and our police surgeon, Dr Horrocks. I left the scene of the tragedy with a constable in charge. It is a good stretch from here - about three miles across the moor.'
'A good walk after breakfast is just what Watson and I need.'
'I had best stay here and give some comfort to the staff.'
I presume she had a next of kin, Sir Henry?'
'There is an aged aunt in Bovey Tracey, I believe. I shall get Barrymore to find her address and then I shall telegraph her. My driver can bring her over to Bovey Tracey so that she can identify the body.'
And thus agreed, Holmes, Merrivale an I donned our souwesters and boots and walked out into the biting October wind.

Chapter Six

Stippledown Rocks was an ancient quarry, accessible only by foot, lying some three miles east of Baskerville Hall. By the time we reached our destination it was already approaching mid morning. The rain had eased, some of the dense mist had cleared and a pale, watery sun peeked from behind grey clouds. Gingerly, we climbed down the side of the quarry, slipping every so often on the wet shale. At last we entered a deep gully where a space had been marked out with a series of metal poles and a red and white ribbon, guarded by a disconsolate constable.
'Alright, Stevens, you can take a break,' Merrivale instructed.

Holmes, who had been unusually reticent that morning, suddenly appeared animated on reaching the scene of the tragedy. Tape measure in hand, he began examining the ground where the body had lain in great detail but saying not a word to us. Merrivale and I had smoked half a cigar each when Holmes stood up suddenly, made a note in his pocket book and said:
'I believe that there is little more that I can do here, gentlemen.'
'You have found evidence?' asked Merrivale.
'I have examined the footprints. There are in fact no less than ten prints. There were two people here, one considerably smaller than the other, one older than the

other. One, the smaller of the two, was running for her life when she reached the edge of the cliff.'

'How do you know all this?'

'As regards the length of the step it may be stated that the taller the person, the bigger the stride, except where infirmity or some muscular difficulty predominates. As a useful guide, I have observed that the average length of pace for a person walking unhurriedly approximates to 28 inches, while that of a brisk pace is on average about 32 inches. A fast sprint approximates to something like 40 inches. It has also been observed that the pace shortens with age. The pace of a man of 40 years is about 30 inches while in a man of 30 it is usually about 33 inches. This man is in his 30's.

'In addition to this evidence, there is the question about the woman's method of walking. A slightly spreadeagled walk, which applies here, may mean a number of things. The oscillations in the walk may be due to obesity or even pregnancy, for in both cases the centre of gravity is pitched forwards of its customary position, so the soles must compensate by turning *outwards* in order to give the legs a firmer hold. As we know, the victim was not obese…'

'So Sophie Richards was pregnant?' I asked.

'Indeed, though not quite at the end of her gestation, for the oscillations are not extreme.'

'I am amazed that you can get all that from such a brief examination,' said Merrivale. 'I did not see half of that.'

'You see, but you do not observe.'

Merrivale's face reddened.

'That's putting it bluntly, Mr Holmes.'

'The only spillage of blood here relates to the victim's head trauma. Did you have a chance to examine the body in any detail, inspector?'

'I made a cursory examination.'

'And did you come to any conclusions?'

'That the cause of death was a spinal fracture or a head trauma.'

'We cannot assume that is the case. Indeed it is more likely that she was already unconscious when she reached the edge of the cliff.'

'What makes you say that?'

'From the footmarks nearest to the edge, which are deeply furrowed, showing that she had been dragged there. When a person is unconscious, more dead weight is shifted to the legs. I should like to examine the body in more detail, inspector, if that is possible.'

'Entirely. It's at the morgue in Princetown.'

'But first, I suggest that we return to Baskerville Hall where we Watson and I can inform Sir Henry of the fate of his servant. I also have a few questions to put to him.'

After lunch had been concluded, we retired to the study to smoke cigars. Sir Henry, who was in sombre mood and looked drawn, sat by the fireside in a large pilot's chair.

'This is a wretched, wretched business, Mr Holmes. Who on earth would have done such a dreadful thing?'

'That is yet to be determined,' replied Holmes. 'Tell me, Sir Henry, how well did you know Sophie Richards?'

'As I believe I have already told you, she was a charming and very biddable young lady.'

'That is an interesting choice of words.'
'What are you implying, Mr Holmes?'
'That there was something unusual about you relationship with her.'
'What the heck do you mean?'
'I am suggesting that you had more than a paternal interest in her?'
Sir Henry's face reddened.
'Dammit, Holmes, you are too clever for your own good.'
'In fact, your relationship with her was of a sexual nature.'
'It wasn't like that.'
'Really? Frankly, I find that hard to believe.'
'Alright, I'll admit that we made love.'
'On a regular basis?'
'Whenever we could. I have already told you of my condition.'
'Your satyriasis?'
'Yes, call it what you like. When I am in the grip of this thing, I become insatiable. I am beyond all reason. I cannot stop myself until my appetite is sated. Sophie helped me. I have told you that she was biddable. She showed me great affection, more than Beryl ever did. Beryl was never as understanding about such matters. Women from the Costa Rica are of a different temperament. They are not temperamentally suited to philandery.'
'Indeed.'
'I found that Sophie was sympathetic to my condition and someone I could talk to in complete confidence. She would never divulge my secret. She described it as 'my medical problem,' and offered to assist me. At first, it was merely a case of relieving me. But then matters progressed. There

was, I will admit to you, a chemistry between us. Our relationship was, for a long time, merely platonic. She was well educated for one of her humble status but Sophie was intelligent and well read. In my country, Mr Holmes, we do not have the barriers to different classes that you have here in England. One thing soon led to another and well… you know how it is. First it was just an innocent kiss, then something more than that. You must understand that the ball was not solely in my court. Sophie was what we Canadians describe as 'hot.' Well, gentlemen, I soon found out to my surprise that she was not just hot, but also well practiced in the arts of Venus. Matters between us progressed, and she would visit my room on a nightly basis. I asked her - God forgive me, Mr Holmes, I am ashamed to say it - I asked her to punish me, to drive the lust out of me. But the punishment merely served to heighten my excitement. And there I was, back at the beginning again!'

Sir Henry paused, then wiped his forehead and knocked back his whisky.
'I tell you these things in confidence, Mr Holmes. I would not want Beryl to know of it.'
'You have my word on that. You may count on it.'
'And I,' I added.
'You are both men of the world, and I am sure you will be discreet.'
'Tell me, did Sophie come to your bedroom last night?'
'She did.'
'And at what time did she leave you?'

'I'm not entirely sure. Before dawn, for she was gone by the time I next woke, for I recall seeing the sun rise.'

'Did she ever mention to you the name of another man with whom she was romantically linked?'

'Not that I recall. She had an elderly aunt who she would visit on her day off.'

'In Bovey Tracey.'

' I believe so, yes. She never missed a visit. She was quite devoted to her.'

'And the name and address of this ancient relative?'

'She only ever mentioned her by her first name, Jenny. She lived not far from the town centre, in Pound Street, I think I remember her telling me. Yes, that was it. I used to give Sophie a few pounds every week to help sustain the poor old thing. Mr Holmes, do you reckon this has anything to do with the whereabouts of Beryl?'

'It may have some bearing on the matter. Sir Henry, how certain are you that your wife knew nothing of your nocturnal activities?'

'I am confident that she did not know. Beryl had taken to using one of the bedrooms in the old east wing of the Manor.'

'Oh? Why was that?'

'She found my need for nightly consummation unnatural. I found that my desires became uncontrollable. Beryl found that she could no longer sleep, so she had little option in the matter.'

'Would it not have been wiser to have confided in her regarding your condition?'

'On reflection, yes, I guess so. But I could not bear to tell her.'

There was a long pause. Holmes, who had taken up residence by the fireplace during this interchange, knocked out the ashes from his brier, then, refilling it with his abominable shag, lit its contents and sent a plume of grey smoke into the air.

'I must thank you for your frankness in this matter.'

'I am only too happy to assist you, in any way I can. Who would do such a thing to poor Sophie?'

'It is precisely that which we are endeavouring to answer.'

'What do you intend doing next?'

'First, I should like to examine the servants' quarters. I also wish to speak to members of your staff. Who would you say knew Sophie best?'

'Cook was closest to her. That's Mrs Frazer. Barrymore had less to do with her, of course, being older, quite reserved and of a superior rank. Oh, and there is Tom Marley, our gardener and handyman. I know for a fact that there was some history between them.'

'In what sense?'

'Sophie had a brief dalliance with Tom about sixteen moths ago. He is a good looking chap - very fit and with dashing black curly hair. Very Byronic and a draw for the ladies of the village. Rumour has it, he has not always served them well.'

'So, let us begin with Mrs Frazer.'

'I'm shocked to think of that poor girl, lying out there on the moor. She may have had her faults, sir, but Lord knows she never deserved such a terrible fate.'

Mrs Frazer wiped the tears from her chubby face with a flour spattered hand, leaving two long white streaks on each cheek.

'Tell me about Sophie,' said Holmes in a warm friendly voice, which he often reserved for his female clients.

'She were always a bright girl, too bright, some might say. She had a charming way about her, did Sophie, she could talk to anyone, whatever walk of life. Several young men in Fernworthy would have given their right hand to marry her.'

'She had offers of marriage?'

'She might have for all I know, but she never once consented. She had more sense than to do that.'

'How did she get on with Sir Henry and Mrs Baskerville?'

'She seemed to please the Master. He once said she were 'like a breath of fresh air' about the place, though I'm not too sure about Mrs B.'

'They didn't see eye to eye, then?'

'Oh, she never made a complaint about her, nothing like that. It were that the Mistress often used to turn away from Sophie when she were helping Mr Barrymore serve at table. A woman notices these things. Then there were that business of the missing papers.'

'Missing papers?'

'Some papers - personal stuff, I'm not sure exactly what - disappeared from the Master's study. The Mistress accused Sophie of taking them because she had been last in the study, having laid a fire in there, as she usually did at that time of the day. But Sarah denied everything.'

'I believe Sarah had an elderly aunt who she used to visit on her day off?'

'She never spoke about her to me. I really don't know.'
'She never mentioned her by name?'
'Not that I can recall, sir.'
'Thank you, Mrs Frazer. You have been very helpful. And now, I must ask you to show me Sarah's room.'

We were led by Cook up a narrow staircase into a small airless room at the back of the west wing containing an iron bed, a wash stand and jug, and a small chest of drawers. Through this, Holmes rummaged. From the bottom drawer, he pulled out a gold necklace set with precious stones.
'An expensive item for a servant to have,' he commented.
'Perhaps it is an heirloom?'
'Tell me, Mrs Frazer, did Sarah ever show you this?'
'No, I've never set eyes on it.'
'Indeed, that is interesting. Pass me that lamp, Watson.'
I did as he instructed and Holmes examined the necklace with his lens.
'There is an inscription here: S Perez, C.B.'
'Who, I wonder, might that be?'
'It is the name of the maker.'
'And the C.B?'
'Costa Brava.'

Tom Marley was a tall, well built man in his twenties. His curly dark hair, strong muscled arms, full - set beard and sallow skin gave him a striking look and I was not surprised about Sir Henry's description of him as being something of a Lothario.

'Do have a seat, Mr Marley.'
'This about Sophie, I take it?'
'I have a few questions for you.'
'Happy to oblige.'
Marley stretched his long legs and clasped his hands behind his head.
'First of all, I'd like to know more about you and Sophie.'
'What's there to tell. We were close for a while.'
'How close?'
'We were lovers - for a while. Then things changed.'
'Changed? In what way?'
'She began to make excuses.'
'Excuses about what?'
'About me and her - you know - in the bedroom.'
'I understand. Why do you think that was?'
'I found out by chance. I came back from the Turpin quite late…'
'The Turpin being a public house?'
'My local. They serve strong beer there and I like the crib.'
'Please continue.'
'Anyway, I came back through the yew alley and heard something in the bushes. Well, thinking it might be a burglar, I crept forwards and looked. Just then the moon came out from behind a cloud and I could see them clearly, going at it like a couple of rabbits on heat.'
'*Who* was at it? Be more specific.'
'Why, the Master and Sarah. Both in their birthday suits, her on top. I stayed still for quite a stretch while they carried on with their game. I could see her…'
'Yes, I think I can fill in the picture, Mr Marley. What was your reaction?'

'At first I was angry.'
'Did you confront her about the event?'
'I did not.'
'Did you speak to her employer about it?'
'No, not at first.''
'And then I suppose you conceived the idea of blackmailing him?'
'Who told you that I did?'
'So you don't deny it?'
'I asked him if I might have a raise. When he refused, I gave him some advice. Then he changed his tack.'
'So it was blackmail then?'
'I simply put it to him that his wife might wish to know about what he got up to in the wee small hours.'
'Very well, Mr Marley. I think I have heard enough. You may return to your duties.'

After Marley left I turned to Holmes.
'What do you make of him?'
'A dislikeable lout and an opportunist, but not our quarry. This case is a little more complex than I had anticipated. Come, Watson, we shall visit the mortuary at Princetown and see what evidence we can glean there. '

It was almost midday by the time Holmes had finished interviewing Marley. Our journey to Princetown, the largest of the moorland habitations, passed through rolling valleys, bogs, wetland, and waterfalls. From the back of our fly I glimpsed well trodden paths, ancient, eerie forests and the tumbled ruins of Bronze Age settlements, inhabited in an age when the climate was more hospitable.

The Baskerville Papers

The town itself, set high above the surrounding countryside, was a rather grim place of grey, granite buildings, with its forbidding prison housing some eight hundred, long term prisoners.

The Princetown morgue was housed in a tall, dark building on the edge of town. A constable let us in and we entered a narrow vestibule which smelt strongly of formaldehyde. A tall, stooped figure with curly grey hair and beard was bent low over a white fleshed cadaver.

'Mr Sherlock Holmes?'
'And this is his companion, Dr Watson,' Lestrade explained.
'A pleasure to meet you both. I have read much of your exploits in The Strand Magazine.'
'Quite so,' replied Holmes, rather brusquely. 'This is the body of Sophie Richards, I assume?'
'Yes it is. Quite a looker, by all accounts.'
I looked down at the body and saw a tall, athletic figure with long, lustrous hair, slender neck, full breasts and pronounced *mons veneris*. The strange, pale flesh of the corpse, with its v shaped incisions and crude cat gut sewings, denoted the mark of the pathologist.
Holmes picked up the left hand and examined it with his lens.
'Hmm. Interesting.'
'What is?' asked Dr Horrocks.
'These epidermal traces under the fingernails. She put up something of a fight before her attacker must have overwhelmed her.'

'She was pregnant. About three month's gestation, I would suggest.'

'You are correct. And she has been violated, I observe. See here, Lestrade, these tears on the labia? I would suggest that she was also attacked with a blunt wooden implement. Post mortem.'

'How do you know that?' I enquired.

'Because the flesh tears are much redder in hue.'

'That is correct, Mr Holmes. There are two flesh tears in the vaginal wall. In addition, I also found three bite marks, one on the lower abdomen, one on the neck and one on the left buttock,' observed Dr Horrocks.

'These are entirely different in hue. They were administered whilst the victim was still alive. That suggests the victim may have indulged in some sexual foreplay, though not necessarily with her attacker. Cause of death?'

'Cardiac arrest, caused by the asphyxia, induced by strangulation.'

'I concur. I note she was garrotted. Interesting. I'll wager that the same rope was used as in the Smith case. It is of the same width, judging by these indentations to the neck.'

Holmes leaned over the corpse again and sniffed.

'Laudanum, if I am not mistaken. And...patchouli oil. Well, that appears to be everything of importance. Except...Halloa? What's this?' he exclaimed, holding up the victim's right hand. He held up a long grey hair which glistened in the light. Again, Holmes sniffed. 'Gentleman's pomade - and of expensive quality. A detail, but one of significance, Lestrade. What about the victim's clothes and possessions?'

Dr Horrocks went into a small room at the back of the mortuary and returned, bearing a large cloth bag, whose contents he lay before us: a mud spattered, floral cotton dress, a pair of bloodstained red knickers, a pair of black court shoes, two stained silk stockings and a small tartan patterned evening bag, containing a purse. Holmes leaned forward to examine the objects, then opened the purse. Inside was a pound note, some loose change and a crumpled piece of paper which he straightened on the table.

'Meet tonight, 11.30pm, Stippledown Rocks, J.' he read out.

'Written in the murderer's own hand,' I observed.

'The handwriting is interesting,' Holmes replied.

'What do you deduce from it?' asked Lestrade.

'The study of handwriting is far from being an exact science and this is but a small sample. However, there are some interesting features. It is written by a man, that part is obvious. But note the tense handwriting, the extremely strong pressure used. Then there is separation of words and narrowness. You may also note, Lestrade, the emphasised upper zones and the left of upright slant. I have the strong impression, gentlemen, that we may be dealing with a sadistic murderer. Thank you, Dr Horrocks, you have been most helpful. And now, I think, some lunch, gentlemen. I seem to recall The Red Lion in Barrack Street does an excellent roast meal.'

Chapter 7

The following morning I rose late, from a vivid dream about Rachael, the young woman I had encountered at the music hall. Modesty forbids me from describing the precise and very intimate content of the dream. Suffice it to say that my carnal wishes regarding this lady were fully realised, which gave me much joy - that is, until I awoke, dressed, then looked out of my bedroom window. A thick October mist had wrapped itself about the moor, so impenetrable that I could barely make out the shapes of the trees that clustered about the yew alley where the former resident of Baskerville Hall, Sir Charles, had expired from heart failure.

Holmes and I had finished our breakfast and were seated around a roaring fire in the study, smoking our pipes. For a few minutes, my companion said nothing but slumped in his chair, his eyes closed, his head wreathed in pipe smoke. I knew better than to disturb him when he was in this state, for experience has taught me that at such times, his cognitive faculties were at full stretch. At last I broke the silence.

'Have you any idea who our murderer might be?' I enquired tentatively.
'I have a few suspicions. However, they are not based on sound evidence. I would be happy to hear your views, though, my dear fellow.'
'Well, there is one thing which seems significant in the case of the maid, Sophie.'

'Oh, and pray, what is that? he replied.
'Why, the method of murder. She and Smith were both violated in a particularly brutal way.'
'And because of this, you conjecture that both were killed by the same person?'
'I do. Is it not a reasonable theory?'
'Yes, if you are willing to admit that it is merely one of many possible theories. However, Watson, you have not suggested a motive. And you may remember also that in the case of Smith, the murderer certainly had two accomplices.'
'Perhaps both victims may have been killed by a woman for sadistic pleasure?'
'Watson, this is mere fantasy and we cannot regard it as significant. As for our victims, we also have a gender difference.'
'But is it not still a *possibility* that Sophie may have been murdered by a female assailant?'
'It is very doubtful. Women do not usually wear gentlemen's pomade. Besides, in the history of crime, only about ten per cent of such sexually inspired murderers have been women, and of those that were, young children were their targets. You are, I presume, imagining that Beryl Baskerville is our murderer?'
'Yes, it had occurred to me. Perhaps she found out that her husband had committed adultery, sought revenge and lured her onto the Moor. She is, in Sir Henry's own words, a passionate being. Filled with horror at what she had done, she then fled the scene. Have you been able yet to build a clearer picture of Sophie's killer?'

'There are as yet few clues. I am certain only of these facts: that her attacker was almost certainly a man, used expensive hair cream, and that he also was aged about thirty and smoked cigars. We do know he was known to Sophie Richards and that for some reason she visited him in Bovey Tracey. What is not clear to me is the nature of their relationship and her desire for secrecy.'

Holmes was about to add something further when we were interrupted by a knock on the door.

'Yes, Mrs Frazer, what is it?'

'Beg pardon, sir, but after our chat together on Wednesday, something occurred to me about Miss Richards.'

'Go on.'

'Well, the Tuesday evening before we found her missing…'

'The evening of the twenty third.'

'Yes, sir. Well, I had gone out to the scullery to get the mop, and as I opened the back door, I thought I could hear voices. One of them was Sophie's, I was sure of it.'

'And the other? A man or a woman?'

'Oh, it was a man.'

'And how would you describe the man's voice? Was it deep or high? A younger or older person's?'

'High I would describe it as, and not an old voice. Why, not uncommonly like yours, sir.'

Holmes smiled.

'And from which direction did the voices come?'

'From the top of the yew alley.'

'Not more than fifty yards away.'

'Was the man's voice at all familiar to you? Could it have been Sir Henry's voice?'

'I don't think it was Sir Henry's. Now you mention it, I may have heard it before, but it was a while ago, I should say.'
'But may it have been someone you know who came to the Hall - a visitor, perhaps.'
'Yes, it might be.' Mrs Frazer frowned as she delved into her memory.
'No matter. Try not to vex over it and your memory of the event may eventually return to you. I am grateful to you.'
Mrs Frazer, looking pleased, curtsied, then left the room.

We had barely been alone for ten minutes and had both begun loading our pipes, when there was another knock on the door. A ruddy cheeked Dr Mortimer stood in the doorway, his glasses smeared with rain water, his greatcoat saturated.
'You came here in haste, doctor,' said Holmes. 'What is the matter?'
'How do you know that?' asked Mortimer, looking mildly surprised.
'The height of the splashes of mud on your left arm indicate it.'
'The weather is beastly, is it not? First, the fog, then this torrential rain. Still, that is always the way with moorland weather.'
'Come, warm yourself by the fire for a moment or two. Watson, the brandy.'
I obliged and in a few minutes the good doctor seemed to revive.
'A piece of information has come my way regarding Beryl's disappearance.'

'Indeed. Please elaborate.'

Holmes dipped a spill into the fire and lit his pipe. Soon the room was wreathed in clouds of blue smoke.

'Yesterday morning I travelled by train to Exeter to see my solicitor. When I arrived back at Bovey Tracey late afternoon, one of the railway staff stopped me and informed me that he had some information which might have a bearing on Beryl's disappearance. At shortly after two pm some days after Beryl was reported missing, he saw something which he found rather disturbing. As the London train was about to depart, he saw three people on the platform - two men and a woman. At first he thought that they were agitated because they were afraid of missing the train, for he had just blown the whistle. But then it occurred to him that something else was actually taking place. The two men must have been pushing the woman onto the train into a first class apartment. Then the two men also climbed aboard, shutting the door after them. He said that, judging by her reactions, the woman seemed as if she were drunk.'

'You took the man's name and address, I take it?'

Mortimer nodded and handed a sheet of paper to Holmes.

'Grimpen village. That is but a twenty minute ride from here. I shall drop in to see the fellow this evening on his return from work.'

I was about to retire after one of Mrs Frazer's sumptuous dinners when I heard the rattle of carriage wheels on the cobbled yard. Holmes soon appeared, looking pale and weary, and it occurred to me that since my remonstrance with him about the morphine he had quite clearly continued his regime of self abuse.

'Still up, Watson? Then do me the kindness of pouring me a stiff brandy, would you?'
'Did you have any luck with Mr Yeoman?'
'The station master was a sprightly, somewhat garrulous fellow but his recollections were dimmed by the quantity of Scotch whisky he had consumed after his return from work. He could not give me the precise date when he witnessed the little pantomime on the platform, neither could he describe in detail to me the appearance of the three participants, save that one of the men was taller than the other and wore a black ulster and a bowler. The woman was shorter than the men and had curly black hair. All of which gets us no further towards reaching a solution.'
'Do you fear that Beryl Baskerville has been abducted?' I asked.
'I am sure of it, though I cannot yet say by whom. And for what purpose, since there has been no request yet for a ransom? These are dark days, Watson, and I fear there are more yet to come.'

After Mortimer had left us, Holmes and I donned our mackintoshes and wellingtons and took the footpath across the Moor to Stippledown rocks. The rain had ceased at last, leaving a sky bruised by dark clouds and a misty horizon. Holmes was in sombre mood and had retreated into silence, so that I was able to observe the landscape in more detail. There were few signs of human habitation, except for the occasional derelict cottage or tumbled cairn. Our path wound between the huts once occupied by early Britons, who had farmed here in warmer and more hospitable climes, then onwards, past the great Grimpen Mire, where we had seen the last of the evil Stapleton. Then we were climbing steadily up a low hill to the old quarry site at Stippledown. As we stood on the brow of the hill, looking down, Holmes suddenly broke his silence.

'Have you ever heard of the term, 'genius loci,' Watson?'
'The spirit of place, if my Latin is correct.'
'It is correct. The notion that each place in the landscape is accompanied by its own spirit. A purely irrational idea but one that I still find attractive, nonetheless. This place surely possesses one, but it is a dark, malign spirit which threatens to corrode the lives of many who come here.'
'And yet, when the sun is shining, the Moor can be a place of great beauty,' I observed.
'Eminently sensible. Perhaps I have spent too much of my life looking through a glass darkly.'
'You have encountered much human cruelty and iniquity. Your reaction is hardly surprising.'
'Yet there is a force at work here, a primal force, to which the human spirit responds. Come, Watson, there is nothing further here that can help us in our quest. The rain has done its worse to confound us and succeeded. The matter remains a conundrum.'
And so saying, we trudged our way back to Baskerville Hall.

I spent a sleepless night, tossing and turning. Shortly after eleven o'clock, a strong sou'westerly had risen and with it came a high wind. It roared and moaned its way down the chimneys of the old Hall, tugging at tapestries and rattling the window panes. At around three o'clock, I rose from my bed and, drawing the heavy curtains, peered out into the blackness. I had not stood there very long before I became aware of two small lights bobbing up and down. I estimated that two people must be walking across the Moor, carrying lanterns. What and who would be out walking at this ungodly hour, I reasoned? There was not a single habitation within three miles, unless someone was bivouacing in one of the ancient huts near Grimpen Mire. And there had been no reports of escaped prisoners, as far as I knew.

I rose late the following morning, weary and troubled by strange dreams. In one of these, I was standing on the edge of the quarry at Stippledown Rocks, when I felt someone push me hard in the back. Losing my footing, I felt myself falling and before my head made contact with the ground I caught a glimpse of Holmes. He was standing at the edge, his hand around the neck of Beryl Baskerville. 'I have looked through the glass,' he said, 'and can see only darkness.'

Holmes, Sir Henry and I had barely finished our breakfasts when Barrymore appeared.
'Sorry to interrupt your breakfast, Sir Henry, but Inspector Merrivale has arrived. He seemed very anxious to talk to Mr Holmes. Shall I ask him to wait in the study?'
'No, Barrymore, show him right in. I am hoping this is good news, gentlemen.'

Barrymore nodded and left. Within a minute, Merrivale appeared, looking windswept and somewhat weary.

'Tell me that you have found Beryl, Inspector,' said Sir Henry.

'I am afraid not, sir. Rather sad news I'm afraid. I believe your wife is a friend of Laura Lyons of Bovey Tracey?'

'Indeed. She was also a friend of Sir Charles. Has some misfortune happened to her?'

'I am sorry to inform you that her body was discovered early this morning at her home. We believe she has been murdered.'

I was aware that Holmes had risen to his feet and was peering across at Merrivale with an expression of mixed anger and alarm.

'At what time was this?'

'Seven o'clock. She was discovered by a neighbour. She had gone in through the back door of the cottage. She had become concerned because she had not seen Miss Lyons for some days.'

'And how did she die?'

'We are not entirely sure at present, Mr Holmes. The doctor thought it might have been poison, but he can't be entirely certain. The police surgeon, Dr Horrocks, is presently carrying out an autopsy on the body over in Princetown.'

'In which room was she discovered?'

'Under the stairs.'

'The stairs?'

'Yes, Mr Holmes. In the cupboard under the stairs. She was also naked. Miss Lacey, the neighbour, opened the door because of the smell coming from there.'

'That's mighty weird,' observed Sir Henry.
'I should like to see the house and visit the mortuary,' said Holmes.
'I shall certainly arrange it. How about this afternoon, around two? I can't be there since I have a court appearance. But I will inform uniformed. I would appreciate any help you can offer me with this one. I have rather a heavy case load at present.'
'Happy to oblige, Inspector.'

Holmes gave the mortuary doorbell a rigorous pull and very soon after, a red faced Dr Horrocks answered our summons.
'Come in, gentlemen, Inspector Merrivale told me you might be dropping by this afternoon. This is becoming something of a habit, I must say.'
I noticed that his eyes were bloodshot and there was a smell of spirits on his breath.
'This one came in earlier this morning,' said Horrocks. Opening one of the mortuary hatches, he wheeled out the body onto a gurney like a costermonger wheeling out a trolley full of fruit. Immediately, my nostrils were assailed by the smell of rotting flesh.
'Sorry about the stench. She's a few days old and even at this time of the year, the process of decay can be quite rapid. You'll notice the slight green hue of the head and bloating of the face.'
'More than thirty six hours?' replied Holmes.
'About that, though we should allow for the fact that she had been stuffed into a cupboard.'

'Merrivale informs me that you have yet to determine the cause of death.'

'That is proving a little difficult, I will admit. I suspect it was some sort of poison, though you will probably also notice the chafing to the wrists.'

Holmes nodded.

'Indicating that she was tied up…And tortured. See these marks here on the breasts and abdomen, Watson?'

'Cigarette burns.'

'No, these are wider, more irregular than cigarette burns. A cigar.'

'I thought as much myself,' said Horrocks.

Holmes sniffed the corpse's lips, then frowned.

'Certainly not an alkaloid substance. You examined the stomach contents?'

'Not much to look at. She had voided most of her stomach contents onto the carpet.'

'Which you also have examined?'

'Naturally. No leads there, either. She ate a roast beef dinner with vegetables about two hours before she died. There was also alcohol in her bloodstream.'

'That would mean she died late on Saturday evening, around nine o'clock. And no evidence of a toxin?'

'None that I could perceive, though you may have more luck than me.'

'That would require further tests.'

'You are most welcome to use my resources,' said Dr Horrocks.

Although Holmes spent over an hour examining the body of Laura Lyons, he discovered little more that was of use to him that afternoon. We thanked Dr Horrocks, climbed back up into our cab and Holmes instructed our driver, Tom Marley, to take us directly to Bovey Tracey.

The residence of Laura Lyons was one of a row of small terraced cottages situated not far from the railway station. Outside the house in question we found a solitary constable who, by the redness of his face, had probably been on duty there for some considerable time. Merrivale, on hearing our approach, appeared in the doorway, wrapped in greatcoat and thick woollen scarf.

'Come in, gentlemen, everything is as it was first found to be. Nothing has been tampered with, I can assure you.'

'I am glad to hear that, Inspector,' said Holmes, looking around the room. Suddenly, he went down on all fours and began examining the carpet of the lounge and hallway with his lens. After a few minutes of this, he stood up and made a few notes in a small pocket book.

'Has anything been removed from this room, Inspector? Any of the victim's personal possessions, for example?'

'Yes. We have the woman's dress and under garments. Also her handbag.'

'I should like to examine these.'

'Certainly. Constable Crabbe!'

'Yes, sir?'

'Ask Jenkins to relieve your post and bring me the two evidence bags.'

'Yes, sir.'

Looking relieved, PC Crabbe disappeared down the hallway, then returned carrying three large brown paper bags. Holmes opened the first of these and pulled out a floral patterned dress. Then he opened the second bag, which contained a pair of silk stockings, a pair of red camisole knickers and a black shift.

'Interesting. See these stains, Watson? Evidently Miss Lyons had sexual intercourse prior to her death.'

'Consensual?'

'I think not, judging by the rip in her underwear. And there are two bloodstains on the shift, here and here. No, I would say this is a violent assault.'

Holmes opened the third bag which contained a large brown handbag. From it, he extracted first a bundle of letters which he rapidly perused, a black journal, then a folded piece of writing paper. He opened the sheet and read aloud:

'For whom it may concern: I have decided to leave this cruel, stale and empty world, for I can no longer bear it without my love. Do not think badly of me, B. We shall meet again in the Summerlands. LL.'

'What do you make of it?' Merrivale asked.

'It's quite clearly a forgery.'

'Why do you say that?'

'Look at the handwriting. It is clearly different from that of her letters here. A good imitation, mind, but not quite good enough. The e's are quite different as is the slope of the hand, which in the letters is much more to the right. Tell me, did you find any hairs on the undergarments?'

'Several, all of them pubic hairs, belonging to the victim.'

'I should like to examine them. Tomorrow perhaps. Now, I think I have all that I need for the moment, Inspector. May I retain this journal and the letters?'

'Certainly, Mr Holmes. So long as you return them to me before you go back to London.'
'I am happy to oblige.'

We drove back to the Hall amidst a thunderstorm which banged and rattled its way across the ink black skies. Holmes sat in the back of the carriage, turning the pages of the diary until, at last, the skies opened and heavy, torrential rain forced him to push the volume deep into his inner coat pocket. When we arrived back, Barrymore was standing beneath the porch, holding a large black umbrella.
'Sir Henry, you have a visitor.'
'Oh, who?'
'Mr Frankland. He is waiting in the study.'
'Very well. Show him into the lounge whilst we get these wet coats off our backs. It never rained quite like this back home, that's for sure!'
It was some years since I had set eyes on old Frankland. He had aged considerably. The jagged eyebrows seemed more pronounced, the hawk nose mapped with more lines and the eyes had turned almost milky white. It was the countenance of a weary and embittered man.
He rose to shake Holmes' hand.
'A dreadful business, Mr Holmes. Dreadful! Have you any notion as to who might have committed such cruelty on my poor daughter?'
'These are early days, Mr Frankland. However, I am sorry for your loss. The death of a child is always the hardest of all to bear.'
'Would you care for some tea, Frankland?' said Sir Henry.
'A double scotch would help matters.'

Sir Henry rang the servant's bell and Barrymore appeared.
'A bottle of our best malt, Barrymore, and three glasses. And now, gentlemen, you must forgive me but I have some urgent business to attend to.'
'What I should like to know is, why was she naked?' asked Frankland after our glasses had been duly charged and Sir Henry had left the room.
'The probability is that the murderer removed her clothes because he was sexually motivated. I believe she knew her assailant and invited him in.'
'How can you be sure of that?'
'Because neither the front nor the back door had been forced.'
'So if it was not a stranger who she admitted, it must, as you suggest, have been a man - and someone in her social circle. I find that unlikely.'
'Why so?'
'Because she was a follower of Sappho and her detestable kind.'
Holmes raised an eyebrow at me.
'You mean that your daughter was a lesbian?'
'That is not a word I like to hear, Mr Holmes, let alone think about. Laura was brought up in a sound Christian family. I can only think that she was seduced by this woman, Beryl Baskerville.'
'Why should you assume that?'
'Why, they were never out of each other's company, goddammit! They were involved with this Womens' Mission Centre.'
'The refuge in Bovey Tracey for abused and homeless women?'

'A temple dedicated to female depravity.'
'Was there not once a Mr Lyons?'
'There was, though they parted some two years ago, and not on good terms.'
'He mistreated her?'
'He took a riding crop to her backside on many an occasion, and I applaud the man for it. Why, I used to do the same myself when she was younger. The birch is character building, do you not agree? It stiffens our resolve. Why, man, it's the main building block of our public schools.'
Holmes did not reply.
'Then there were those ghastly paintings.'
'What paintings?' I asked.
'Portraits of Laura in the buff. God knows who painted them or what she got up to in those sessions.'
'Where are these paintings now?' Holmes asked.
'I haven't a clue. She used to keep them in her office out the back where she did most of her secretarial work.'
'They are not there now.'
'Or perhaps we did not see them,' observed Holmes.
'If I set eyes on them again I shall surely burn them.'
'I sincerely hope you do no such thing, Mr Frankland. They may prove to contain valuable evidence. Do you know who the artist was?'
'I have no idea. And when I do get my hands on him, he may expect a horse whipping.'

Chapter 8

The following morning I was late down to breakfast. When I arrived in the breakfast room I found myself quite alone save for an attentive Barrymore and his wife.
'Still short staffed?' I asked Barrymore as he dished out my kedgeree. Barrymore frowned and gave a suppressed cough.
'I believe a young lady is to be interviewed this morning for the post left vacant by Miss Richards.'
'That must be a relief to you both.'
'Indeed, sir. Especially to Mrs Barrymore, who has borne much of the brunt of it.'
'Let us hope that she proves satisfactory then.'
'Miss Richards was more than capable in her duties. It may prove difficult to replace her.'

By nine thirty still no one had appeared in the breakfast room, so I decided to while away some time in the study. There was an impressive and large collection here, comprising both classical and modern works. For some while I sat reading Sir James Richards' impressive account of The Afghan Wars. Then, when I had finished my cigar, I turned my attention to a large cabinet entitled: 'Special Interest Collection: Incunabulae.' Although this appeared locked, I noticed that the key was in the lock, so I opened the door. There were several books by both Roman and Greek authors which I was unfamiliar with, and a tome which immediately caught my eye, entitled: 'Venus In India.' Thinking that this might prove of interest to a retired member of His Majesty's Armed Forces, I sat down in one of the comfortable easy chairs and began reading. The first thing that caught my attention was a small label attached to the front end paper with the inscription, 'The Erotikon Book Club.' This immediately rang a bell and I recalled Holmes mentioning that this was the book club originated by Leonard Smith. I turned to the first page of the narrative and settled myself to read:

'It was in the middle of August when I landed in Bombay, that queenly capital of Western India. The voyage had been unimportant. Our passengers had been few and stupid, chiefly old Indian Civilians and officers returning unwillingly to the scenes of their labours in the hot country, after a short spell of life in England. It was not the season of the year when sprightly young ladies go out to India, each one with the fine hope in her heart that her rounded, youthful charms, her cheeks glowing with health, and her freshness might captivate a husband. We were a staid party: some like myself had left young wives at home: others were accompanied by theirs; all were of an age when time had softened down the burning ardours of passion, and when perhaps the last thought to enter their heads, on retiring at night to rest, was to take advantage of the ruined remains of beauty which reposed by their sides.'

The introduction seemed a little dull, but as I persisted, the text soon took a very different direction:

'The route from Bombay via Allahabad to Peshawar runs almost entirely through a country as flat as a table. At this season of the year, when I traversed it by train, the land lay dry, and the parching weather had apparently not been tempered by the rains, which usually fall between June and September. Here and there stood green waving crops, contrasted with the otherwise generally brown, burnt up soil, and there were few stretches of country which formed such attraction for the eyes as to call for mental appreciation, in comparison with the charms of the beautiful Mlle. De Maupin, especially as painted by Theophile Gautier, in that glowing chapter where she appears in all her milky white skinned, arousing beauty, naked, and burning with tormenting desire, before the eyes of her enraptured lover! Oh, Theophile! Why did you not allow your pen to describe, with a little more freedom, those undraped beauties? Why did you not permit us to do more than fancy the exquisite pleasures which the panting lovers experienced on their voluptuous couch?'

How well I recalled Peshawar, the very area where an Afghan bullet had punctured my subclavian artery and left me with aches, pains and a rheumatic shoulder ever since.

It had now grown warm in the room and, loosening my collar, I read on:

'Oh, dear reader! Just as I opened my eyes I saw, through the half-open door a perfect figure of feminine beauty! A girl clothed in a close fitting grey coloured dress with a Teria hat archly sloped on her lovely and well-shaped head! That beautiful face! How perfect the oval of it! Truly she must have aristocratic blood in her veins to be so daintily formed! What a rosebud of a mouth! What cherry lips! God! Jupiter! Venus! What a form! See those exquisite rounded shoulders, those full and beautiful arms, the shape of each can be so plainly seen, so close does her dress fit her: and how pure, how virgin like is that undulating bosom! See how proudly each swelling breast fills out her modest but still desire-provoking bodice! Ah! The little shell-like ears, fitting so close to the head! How I would like to have the privilege of gently pressing those tiny lobes! What a lovely creature she looks! How refined! How pure! How virginal! Ah! My Louie, like you, this girl is not to be tempted, and long and arduous would be the chase before she could be compelled to own that her failing strength must yield her charms to the hands and lips of her panting pursuer! No! That girl, of all girls I have seen, struck me as one not to be seduced from the path of purity and honour. And all these impressions flashed through my fevered brain.'

I was about to read on with this curious narrative when there was a sound at the study door. Holmes was standing there dressed in his old mouse coloured dressing gown, his favourite meerschaum between his lips.
'Interesting reading, Watson?'
'You might say that, Holmes.' He picked up the volume and examined it closely.
'Charles Devereaux. The author is not familiar to me, I must confess.'
'Nor I.'
'A somewhat demonstrative and loquacious style. Ah, I see now what sort of a narrative this is...' said he, with a wry

smile. 'I have read much that is similar in the back of Smith's bookshop. I assume you noted the bookplate?'

'Do you regard that as significant?'

'It may have some bearing on the case. It appears, then, that Sir Henry has something of a penchant for erotic literature.'

'Do you find that surprising?'

'I do not, considering what we know about his erotomania. But the bookplate is, as you have indicated, a connection to Smith's book club. Is there any of that kedgeree left, Watson?'

'There is, though I fear it has gone cold by now.'

'I have been reading Laura Lyon's letters,' said Holmes as he returned from the side table, with a plate full of kedgeree.

'And what have you discovered?'

'Some of the letters are business correspondence. But the rest are from Beryl Baskerville, the last being dated over a month ago.'

'And their contents?'

'Oh, warm, Watson. Positively steaming.'

'So old Frankland was right about those two?'

'He was. Ah, here is Sir Henry at last.'

Sir Henry had appeared at the door, looking tired and haggard. His shirt collar was askew and his trousers were creased.

'Good morning, Sir Henry. I trust you slept well?' Holmes asked.

'Not very well at all. I should tell you, Mr Holmes, about the curious incident in the night time.'

'What incident?'

'I must have woken around three o'clock. I had been dreaming, a strange, disturbing dream concerning Beryl. I went over to the window and opened it a fraction. It was a light, at some distance away, out on the moors. Who could be out there at such a late hour? Anyway, I went to retrieve my binoculars from the bedside table and by the time I had returned to my post, the light had gone.'

'I too have seen that light,' I said. 'What can it mean, Holmes?'

'It means that there is someone out there who is observing our movements, Watson. And has been ever since we arrived here.'

Holmes turned to Sir Henry. 'However, there is another matter which I should like to raise concerning your wife, Sir Henry.'

'And what is that?'

'A bundle of letters was discovered at Laura Lyon's house. The majority of them had been written by Beryl.'

'I would expect that. They were friends.'

'I think you will find that they were more than friends.'

'What exactly do you mean?'

'That they also enjoyed a physical relationship.'

'I cannot believe that.'

'Then I suggest you read them for yourself.'

'I certainly shall.'

'There are also a number of letters from yourself, Sir Henry.'

Sir Henry's face reddened.

'Yes, I admit that I had some limited business correspondence with Laura.'

'The letters are twenty in number and of a very intimate tone. Shall I read one of them out to you?'
'I prefer it that you do not.'
'Then I shall accede to your wishes.'
'I'll come clean with you on the matter, Mr Holmes. Laura and I had a fling, but it didn't last more than a couple of months at the very most.'
'You were in love with her?'
'Not exactly in love. It was rather more of a physical relationship. Laura was very imaginative in that regard. And I had my needs, as I have already indicated to you.'
'When was this?'
'Some months ago. I was introduced to Laura by Beryl when I was asked to contribute to the Women's Mission.'
'And you visited her at her house in Bovey Tracey?'
'Quite often, yes.'
'Were you aware that Laura had other male visitors?'
'I was aware that she had a few male friends.'
'Laura sat as a life model for a number of paintings. Did you know about this?'
'I knew of it. She had one framed on her study wall.'
'Did you happen to know the artist's name?'
'Laura never told me his full name. She just referred to him as John. I guess he was a local painter. It was done in heavy oils, very Expressionistic in style. A little too explicit for some tastes but I thought it rather fine.'
'He knew her well?'
'I got that impression, yes.'
'Did she visit him at his studio?'

'She never mentioned that he had a studio. Laura also had some high quality photographs done by him. She gave me one of them as a sort of love token.'

'I should like to see it.'

'Of course. I will get it for you. It's in a drawer in the study.'

Sir Henry disappeared into the study as Holmes re-lit his pipe with a long spill.

'You look surprised, Watson.'

'I confess that I am quite shocked.'

'You should not be. After all, Sir Henry has already admitted to his proclivities regarding the fairer sex.'

'Yes, but all the same…'

We were interrupted by Sir Henry's appearance at the door.

'Here are the photographs,' he said cheerily, as if they were a commonplace. Holmes opened the folder and took out three photographs, each measuring five by seven inches. The first showed a buxom Laura Lyons, lying on a tiger skin rug before a roaring fire. Her long dark hair had been draped across her wide back, falling short of her plump buttocks. She was leaning on her arms, her smiling face looking up to the camera. The second photograph had been taken al fresco. It showed a dense piece of woodland which I immediately recognised as the ancient Wistman's Wood. The subject sat on a large boulder, clad only in a pair of tight fitting black cami-knickers. She was leaning forward, her left hand supporting her plump chin. The third portrayed its subject as a dominatrix, dressed in a black corset, silk stockings and thigh length boots. Her left hand held a leather whip.

'Charming, aren't they?' said Sir Henry.
'To a conossieur of erotica,' Holmes replied.
Sir Henry smiled. 'You sound as if you don't approve, Mr Holmes.'
'I do not have a view on the matter. Have you heard of something known as The Erotikon Book Club?'
'Yes, I have been a member of it for over a year now.'
'Are you familiar with its publisher?'
'You mean Leonard Smith?'
'The same.'
'I read he was found dead in his flat?'
'Yes.'
'I met him once at a party in Chelsea. A charming fellow. He has done the reading public a great service.'
'Not according to the National Vigilance Society.'
'Who the Devil are they?'
'They are a body of people intent on the suppression of vice.'
Sir Henry laughed.
'Only in England could there be such a thing! In Canada we have a very different view of such literature. Most of it is harmless stuff, in my view.'
'Do you know if Smith had any enemies?'
'I believe I already told you, Mr Holmes, I did not know him that well. I believe he had both supporters and detractors. That is to be expected.'

Holmes was about to answer this observation when there was a loud knock on the study door.
'Yes, Barrymore, what is it?'
'Telegram for Mr Holmes, sir.'

Holmes stood up and took the telegram.

'It seems that my services are required in London. I shall catch the early train to Paddington, Watson. I should prefer you to stay here with Sir Henry and report back to me via telegram.'

'I am happy to do so. May I know the contents of the telegram?'

'There has been a murder. A telegraph boy in Cleveland Street. Lestrade has asked me to look into the matter.'

'Is not Lestrade capable of dealing with the crime?' asked Sir Henry.

'It is not so straight forward as that,' Holmes said. 'The crime itself is not particularly important. It is, however, significant of a deeper malaise. That is why my presence is required.'

True to his word, Holmes left for London the following morning, a morning that was cloaked in swirling mist. As I stood in the porch, watching the fly disappear into the murk of the driveway, I felt a cold sensation down my back. When the mist and dark closed in on Baskerville Hall, there came a feeling of melancholy and claustrophobia which was hard to explain to someone like Holmes, whose mind was supremely rational. Nevertheless, I knew that he sensed it.

I spent the rest of the day in the study, browsing through the Baskerville collections, and keeping clear of the cabinet which contained Sir Henry's erotic incunabulae. I had been secretly shocked at his bland endorsement of such literature, although after my own reading of The Pearl, I had to admit it had the ability to raise my ardour.

Feeling somewhat despondent at Holmes' departure, I decided to retire early that night. For some while I lay there, musing over the week's events. Could the solution be that Sir Henry had somehow taken leave of his senses and murdered both his wife and her lover? And if so, what connection did that have with the death of Leonard Smith? It seemed to me that there was a link with the subversive literature which both Smith and Sir Henry devoured, but nothing else made much sense to me.

I must have slept deeply, for when I awoke, my fob watch told me it was twelve thirty. I was dimly aware that a sound had woken me, and it was coming from my window. I crept from my bed and, pulling back the curtains, peered out. There was a full moon, partially covered by scudding clouds.

As I watched, the moon passed from behind a cloud into the open and I saw what looked like a large loping dog, padding its way cautiously along the lawn. Every so often it would pause and look upwards, as if sniffing the air for its quarry. Even as I looked, I could detect that there was something extremely odd about the beast. Then, in a flash of recognition, I realised what it was. The dog had no tail. In fact it was not a dog at all but a man.

As the creature reached the end of the ornamental gardens, it must have caught my scent, for it tensed itself and began to growl. I caught a glimpse in the moonlight of a coarse, lined face, the red eyes flashing angrily, the yellow teeth bared in a grotesque rictus. The hands were long and taloned, whilst the head was completely covered in coarse, black hair. Out of this mane appeared a long, wolfish snout. However, what disturbed me most about the awful vision was the demonic intent behind those eyes and the quick, determined pad-pad as the creature bounded towards the water fountain, its arms outstretched, the hands twisting in an odd, spasmodic fashion as if its owner were the victim of epilepsy. Then suddenly it froze, twisting its head sideways, sniffing the night air. In that instant I knew that I was staring down not simply at the body of a man but at some hellish presence, a succubus which had latched itself onto the disordered mind of a man whose fate had been predestined from the moment of his birth.

I pulled the curtains tight shut and collapsed onto the bed, scarcely believing what I had just witnessed. How could it be possible that in the twentieth century, such things were possible? It defied reason and commonsense. Yet I had seen the transformation with my own eyes. In the morning I would go to Bovey Tracey and telegram Holmes to inform him about what I had seen.

I slept late, waking at eight o'clock. Washed and dressed, I made my way down to the breakfast room, where I found a rather uneasy looking Barrymore, accompanied by a tall young woman with luxuriant blonde hair, tucked under her maid's bonnet.

'Will Sir Henry be down shortly, Barrymore?' I asked.

'Sir Henry is indisposed,' he replied. 'He will not be down to breakfast.'

'Nothing serious, I trust?' I persisted.

'No, sir, just a touch of dyspepsia.'

'And I see we have a new member of staff.'

'This is Lucy. She joined us yesterday.'

Lucy curtseyed. She was fresh faced, with long slender hands, a narrow corsetted waist and a swan-like neck. Her eyes were a brilliant blue and her bosom generous. If I had met such a girl in the streets of Peshawar I would have been very pleased with my good fortune.

'May I pour your tea, sir?' said Lucy, with a smile.

'By all means.'

Lucy picked up the teapot. As she leaned across me to pour, I detected a strong whiff of rich, alluring perfume.

I had just picked up my tea cup and was about to say something to Lucy when there was a loud knock on the front door. Barrymore nodded at Lucy, then left us.

'Have you been long in service, Lucy?'

'Not long, sir. In fact this is my first job.'

'What were you doing before this?'

'I was in Shoreditch, sir. I had an h'occupation there.'

'Oh, doing what?'

She was about to answer when the door of the breakfast room was flung wide, admitting a red faced Frankland.

'I have found him, Dr Watson! I have seen our murderer!'

'Calm down, man. Here, sit and catch your breath for a moment, then tell me what has occurred.'

Frankland collapsed into the basket chair, mopping his brow. I fetched him a glass of brandy which he quickly downed.

'It was the telescope, you see. I invested in a more powerful version and had it installed in the tower a week ago.'

I recalled my previous visit here during the business of the hound.

'Anyway, last night, just before retiring, I looked out of my bedroom window - I sleep on the first floor - and I could see, quite clearly, a light shining out on the moors. I decided that, come morning, I would use my new telescope and find out if there was someone bivouacing out there. About half past nine, I spotted a man in a black overcoat and cloth cap, making his way on the old track in the direction of the Grimpen hut circle.'

'Did you recognise this person?'

'No, I can't say that I did.'

'Did you see his face?'

'Only the back of his head.'

'What colour was his hair?'

'Dark hair.'

'Big or slight build?'

'Big I would say.'

'And this is the first time you have seen him?'

'As I said.'

'Then I shall investigate the matter.'

'You require my assistance?'

'No, I shall go alone. Leave it to me, Mr Frankland.'

True to my word, not long after dinner, and close to dusk, I donned my ulster and boots, then made my way along the route I had previously traversed with Holmes, leading to

Grimpen and the ancient Celtic stone huts. In my inner pocket lay my old service revolver, the trusty Adams, which always accompanied me on my expeditions with Holmes. The moor, with its twisted trees and rock strewn, barren hills, is an eerie place even in broad daylight but in semi-darkness it is a truly mysterious and haunted landscape. Although intensely cold, the air was still and windless. The lowering clouds, which had circled the moors all afternoon, had cleared, leaving a virtually cloudless sky. As I drew level with the top of Stippledown Rocks, I stopped briefly to admire the view. The sun was now almost to the horizon, giving a glorious sunset of pinks and reds. It was an awesome view. I imagined what it would have been like for Ancient Man. Then, this land would have been wooded, as far as the eye could see. What ancestral tales would they have told, what rituals did they perform? Was the legend of the phantom hound, that black dog known as the guardian of the underworld, glimpsed here at dusk on All Hallows Eve?

Dismissing such fancies, I made my way along the narrow, muddy track in the direction of the hut circle. The light was falling fast and the interiors of the huts were pitch black and smelt of sheep's droppings. I took out my dark lantern and examined each one in turn. At last I struck lucky. In the very largest of the huts I found a sleeping bag, a tin mug, a small litmus and dark lantern. There were also the remains of a loaf of brown bread, a half eaten apple and a box of vestas. I determined to stay here in the dark until the resident of the hut returned from his nefarious work and I was convinced I would find a solution to this bizarre affair.

Scarce ten minutes had passed when I heard footsteps approaching. I reached into my coat and drew out my revolver. In a flash, someone was upon me, someone with strong, coarse hands and foul breath. He held me tightly by the throat and was squeezing hard, squeezing the life out of me. I struggled hopelessly, then there was nothing but darkness.

The Baskerville Papers

Part Two

Chapter 9

EXTRACT FROM THE LONDON EVENING NEWS, 16TH OCTOBER 1901

The mutilated body of a young boy was discovered earlier this morning in East London in an alleyway behind Dorset Street. The remains of the youth were discovered by a local postman who was on his rounds. So horrific were the boy's injuries that police have had to erect a temporary barrier to block the awful sight from onlookers. By eight thirty a large crowd had assembled, some of whom threw stones at the police and were then arrested. Inspector Lestrade from Scotland Yard, described the murder as 'a most brutal and shocking case,' and urged the local community to co-operate with his officers in finding the attacker.

Dorset Street was recently referred to by The Times newspaper as 'the worst street in London' and was the scene of two other murders last year, both of which involved prostitutes, known in Cockney parlance as 'drabs.' Local opinion is of the view that they were the work of 'Jack The Ripper,' although Scotland Yard does not support this view. Inspector Lestrade told your reporter that he believed the boy's murder was the work of a 'psychopath,' a word originally used by Russian criminologist, Professor Ivan Balinsky to describe a form of moral insanity, which some believe may be genetically transmitted.

Several officers spent the day visiting the slum dwellings which occupy the major part of the street, though their work was hampered by the fact that many of its residents do not live here permanently but are migrants from Europe and Ireland and many of these people do not even speak the English language.

The identity of the murder victim has yet to be established.

THE JOURNAL OF LAURA LYONS, NEE FRANKLAND

September 20th, 1901

I write these words hoping that one day all members of my sex may enjoy the liberty that society and especially men, have so cruelly denied us. In a small way, I hope that I have done a little to relieve the suffering of those poor souls who have shelter and comfort at our Mission Hall here in Bovey Tracey, but this is insignificant compared to the enormous task that confronts those valiant souls who fight for our suffrage and sexual equality. Here I set down the iniquities of male oppression which have afflicted and curtailed my life so that others may learn from my example.

I spent the first few years of my life in northern India, my father being a captain in the British Army. He had married my mother in the summer of '74, she being the daughter of a prosperous Hindu merchant from Calcutta. Indira was, as I recall, a beautiful young woman of only fifteen years, a fact which caused some consternation among my father's fellow officers. One of these, a Captain Andrews, well known as a womaniser, made advances to my mother and was fortunately caught in the act as he was attempting to ravish her, by my father, who whipped him so hard that the attacker spent six weeks recovering in the base camp's sanatorium.

By the summer of '79, when I was four, the battalion moved from Kabul up country to Peshawar, the capital of the Khyber Pakhtunkhwa province.

The battalion then moved beyond Jhelum, having but one mighty river to pass before leaving the bounds of India proper and treading the outskirts of Central Asia, in the valley of the Peshawar. But it took some two or three days and nights of continuous travel, in a dak gharry, before we reached Attock. The dak gharry is a fairly comfortable mode of conveyance, but one becomes tired of the eternal horizontal position which is the only one which gives any comfort to the weary traveller. Crossing the Indus in a boat rowed over a frightful torrent with the roar of the waters, breaking on the rocks below the ferry, was a very exciting incident for me, especially as it happened at night, and the dark gloom added to its magnifying effect. Then again another dak gharry into which my mother and I got, then lay down and went to sleep, not to waken until finally we reached Nowshera.

My father saw action in the second stage of the Afghan War when a force of 10,000 Afghans, under the command of Mohammed Karpur, staged an uprising and attacked British forces near Kabul in December 1879. Despite besieging the British garrison there, the Afghans failed to maintain the Siege, instead shifting focus to Lord Roberts' troops, and this resulted in the collapse of the rebellion. As a result, my father was shot in the right leg and although he recovered, was left with a slight limp.

During this period of my early life, and until I was in my early twenties, my father continued to drink heavily. Some days he would consume as much as an entire bottle of gin and five or six bottles of strong beer and my mother and I would pay heavily for his addiction. On several occasions I saw him hurl my poor mother across the room, and once she broke three ribs as a result of his drink fuelled rages. I never knew whether these dark moods which consumed him were linked to some incident in his early life, for he never once discussed it. All I know is that he had been born in a tenement dwelling in Shoreditch and that his father was a docker and a drunkard.

I was about twelve when my father first began ill-treating me. My father had been shipped home and was living on his army pension and as a consequence, my mother was obliged to take a menial job as a sales assistant at W.H. Smith. At the time we were living in drab lodgings near to the city of Exeter. I had just started my education and was treated by my class mates as something of a freak because of my dark complexion and jet black hair. I acquired a nickname and became known as 'Blackie Frankland.' Nevertheless, I showed my teachers that I was keen to learn and excelled in most subjects save for Mathematics, which I really could not abide.

I remember the incident well, for it is even now etched deeply in my memory. It was the end of the Christmas term and I had been given a plain brown envelope, containing my report. I can see it now: the small lounge with its dingy light, the sad looking paper chains and the small Christmas tree which was all we could afford, since a good proportion of my mother's meagre wages was spent on drink. I got home, having trudged along snow laden roads to find him sleeping off a hangover, as he sat by a smoking fire. He woke up with a start and, bleary eyed, demanded to know the whereabouts of my mother. When I reminded him that it was six o'clock and she was still working he scolded me for my impudence and told me to hand over my school report. After reading through this carefully, he stood up and addressed me thus:

'It has some merits, this report but you have been remiss in your Mathematics.'

'I tried my hardest, papa.'

'Evidently it was not good enough. That, my young filly, deserves a good thrashing!'

So saying, he walked over to the cupboard and took out a long rattan stick whose end had been slit, in order to facilitate more pain.

'Now then, do as you are told, and bend over my knee.'

I did as I was told, my long, luxuriant black hair cascading down by his ankles. Then I felt my petticoats being pulled up.

'And if you make a fuss, my girl, I shall beat you all the harder!'

I bit my lower lip and prepared, but the pain was worse than I had anticipated, for the rattan's deadly ends had struck my nether lips. Then the second and the third blow followed in quick succession. I began to squeal but the rattan only bit harder. At last the beating was concluded and I stood up, my legs quivering, my buttocks hot and stinging. My father told me to wait and left the room, returning almost at once from the bathroom, and holding in his hand a tube of ointment. He told me it was calendula and good for easing bruised skin. Then he ordered me to bend over once more and began to rub my nether regions vigorously. When he had finished he told me not to trouble my mother with what had just occurred.

Despite my vow not to tell mother, I described to her in some detail what had occurred, but she did nothing to defend me, telling me that the matter was entirely of my own making and not to make such a fuss, since she herself had to endure similar beatings from my father on a weekly basis. I was astounded at this revelation. My bedroom was at the back of our house and my parents' at the front, so I would hear nothing.

On the Friday following this occurrence, my father had returned to the house late and as a consequence, immediately woke my mother and me. My mother stood on the landing and complained about the state he was in, which swiftly threw him into a fit of anger. I watched as he bundled my mother into their bedroom and then, from my position on the landing, stood watching through the crack of the door. My father pulled up my mother's night gown, then pushed her roughly on the bed and, with a long riding whip, began laying into her backside. Appalled though I was to see this maltreatment, I remained at my post, half frozen with fear and astonishment. But what followed seemed almost bizarre. No sooner had my father finished the punishment, than he put down the whip and began caressing my mother in a most passionate and intimate way which I would blush to describe in detail. She responded, and, in short, they coupled with much moaning. I was about to return to my own room, when I saw mother whisper into my father's ear. Placing a bolster under his abdomen, he then lay on his front, his legs spread wide and instructed my mother to 'give no mercy.' My mother did as she was told and the whip descended on his rear again and again until his white buttocks had turned bright red.

I determined there and then that I would leave this mad household as soon as it was possible to gain my independence. I worked hard at school and gained good results in all subjects. In my fifth year, I was allowed to learn secretarial and typing skills, at which I excelled.

At the age of eighteen, I was fortunate to be given the post of governess to a family living in Blackheath, London. The location was sufficiently far from my parents to be of some relief to me and the house itself was a fine mansion with gothic pillars, seven bedrooms, a beautiful ornate garden at front and rear, and a delightful, sunny childrens' room. The house was called The Cedars and my employers were Mr and Mrs Neville St Clair. Mr St Clair was a businessman who worked in the city. He would leave the house very early each weekday morning and then return late. He was a handsome man with a brown, weather beaten face. My charges were a bonny, cheerful pair, Donald, aged seven and his older sister, Wendy.

I soon discovered that I had a natural empathy with children and as a consequence, spent some of the happiest days of my life at The Cedars. I even found the time to practise my typing, Mr St Clair giving me the task of annotating his large and impressive library. Then, one warm July day, a tragedy occurred. Mr St Clair disappeared. He left no note as to why, and when his employers were contacted by the police, they claimed Mr St Clair had left their employ some years ago. Days passed and, there being no progress in the matter, Mrs St Clair contacted the consulting detective, Mr Sherlock Holmes of Baker Street. He and his companion arrived one afternoon and spent some considerable time going through my employer's affairs and questioning Mrs St Clair. Mr

Holmes and his friend, Dr Watson, decided to stay the night. I shall always recall the rich, coarse tobacco wafting into the corridor from Mr Holmes' bedroom and Dr Watson's roving, twinkling eyes.

Mr St Clair returned to The Cedars later the following day, looking the worse for wear and dressed in an old shirt and baggy trousers. His wife seemed both angry and relieved, whereas the children were simply overjoyed to see their papa again. I shall never forget their delight as they both rushed down the drive to see him.

Neither Mr nor Mrs St Clair ever explained to me what had befallen Mr St Clair and I did not dare to enquire further. Sadly for me, a month after this event, my employers put The Cedars up for sale and my contract came to an untimely end. I was cast back into the uncaring world with nothing more than my suitcase and a small sum of money which I had been able to save over the two years of my employment.

I had no other option but to enrol with a typing agency. I was most fortunate in being offered a post as secretary to a Mr Holness and his elderly aunt at their mansion on the outskirts of Bodmin. I arrived by train and then fly at The Beeches on a wild September afternoon. The house was something of a neglected Gothic pile, set in large wooded grounds with a large lake and curious folly erected to honour the goddess Venus.

Mr Holness was well dressed and charming on our first meeting, and took my hand as a gentleman should, as I got down from the fly. I noticed at once his sharp blue eyes and well developed physique and felt that there was between us an immediate feeling of attraction.

After the butler had taken in my luggage, I was soon introduced to old Mrs Verity, Mr Holness' aunt. An ancient crone, dressed in a severe looking black dress, she screwed up her wrinkled face and peered at me through her pince-nez.

'So this is your new bit of stuff, I suppose!' she exclaimed. 'No, Sylvia, this is my new secretary, Miss Laura Frankland,' replied Mr Holness. 'And I would ask you to be courteous to her since she will also be staying here in the coach house.'

Old Mrs Verity snorted and returned to the book she had been reading.

'You will have to forgive my aunt. She has not got the full deck of cards.'

I smiled.

'I'm sure we'll get along famously.'

As things turned out, we did not. From the start, it was clear that the old woman was my enemy. She developed a talent for spying on me and within a few days of my arrival, things started disappearing from my room. I said nothing about this to Mr Holness, who demanded that I should call him Frank.

It was about two months later when matters began to get complicated. For several hours each morning, my employer and I would closet ourselves in his study where he would dictate the text of his latest novel. Mr Holness was the author of a number of romantic novels, writing under the name of Cassandra Bright, and had achieved some success in his field. Intrigued by this, I picked one of his works from the study and settled down to read its contents. It told the story of an English rose who was kidnapped by a scheming mulatto and shipped to Arabia. There she was forced to be a member of a sheik's harem, and to endure a variety of abominations by his tribe. The book contained some rather heated passages which surprised me because of their explicit descriptions and I returned it to the bookshelf, feeling somewhat disturbed.

As the autumn proceeded and the copper beeches shed their leaves and rustled in the driveway outside, my typing of the narrative progressed, as did the nature of our relationship. I soon noticed that the central character in Frank's novel bore a close resemblance to myself. Like me, she had luxuriant hair, a full figure and was artistic. She was also, by nature, intensely passionate. Like me, Clarissa Wood - that was her name - had endured a violent father before leaving home at the age of seventeen. She travelled to London by stage coach where she fell among villains and ne'er do wells, ending up in a squalid boarding house in Spitalfields. There she was rescued by Dorian Valence, a distant member of her family, a consulting detective, employed by Clarissa's family, and the two subsequently fall in love. Like Dorian, Frank was tall and handsome with an athletic figure. He also possessed a charming demeanour and had brilliant blue eyes. And, like Frank, Dorian had been an explorer and student of aboriginal tribes.

Our work together was often punctuated by brief conversations between us. These dealt with a wide range of topics, ranging from politics to sport. Frank was surprisingly enlightened, considering his gender, and even approved of the women's suffrage movement - though not their actions. One morning, when the rain beat on the windows, Frank turned to me.

'Have you ever heard of a woman called Sara Baartman?' he asked me.

'I confess I have not.'

'I came across her case when I was doing some research into the Khoisan tribe of South Africa. They were what we call Hottentots.'

'I have heard of them.'

'Sara's life was both bizarre and tragic. She had a rare anatomical condition known as steatopygia. In layman's terms that means 'large buttocks.'

I blushed at his frankness. Although I was familiar with my employer's direct manner, the phrase took me by surprise.

'Anyway,' Frank continued, apparently unaware of my embarrassment, 'she was brought to Britain by a Scottish doctor and exhibited as a freak show attraction under the name Hottentot Venus.'

'How dreadful.'

'Oh, it gets worse, I'm afraid, Laura. In 1814, after Dunlop's death, a man called Henry Taylor brought Baartman to Paris. He sold her to an animal trainer, who made her amuse onlookers who frequented the Palais-Royal. Georges Cuvier, professor of comparative anatomy at the Museum of Natural History, examined Baartman and searched for proof of a so-called missing link between animals and human beings. Poor Sara Baartman lived on in poverty. She died in Paris of an undetermined inflammatory disease in December 1815. After her death, Cuvier dissected her body, and displayed her remains. Her body ended up in the Museum of Man in Paris.'

'That is indeed a sad story.'

'There is much more that I could tell you but I think it would make you blush.'

'You have noticed I blush?'

'I have but did not dare mention it. Now, shall we proceed with Chapter Ten?'

Later that day I sat in my bedroom going over this exchange in my mind. Why had Frank told me this strange story? What did he mean by it? I knew of his interest in aboriginal people, of course, but the narrative of Sara Baartman I found rather disturbing. Could it be that this was some indirect reference to his own predilections regarding the fair sex? I went over to the mirror and casting off my night clothes, stared at my body in the mirror. I have always been proud of my figure which I believe is often described by men as an 'hour glass' figure. I am generously proportioned, possessing a small waist, broad back and an ample rear which curves gracefully outwards. Was Frank giving me an indirect, covert compliment? And what were those things he dare not mention for fear I should blush? Yes, he had noticed my blushing and I thought he rather liked it. I felt flattered. I decided that the following day, before work commenced, I would slip into the study and try and find out more about poor Sara.

The next morning I rose early, washed, dressed and sprayed on my chest a sweet - smelling lavender. The study was lit by the early morning sunlight, which streamed in through the gothic windows. I glanced at the anthropological section and soon came across what I had hoped to find: a slim volume entitled: 'The Hottentot Venus.' I sat down to read it.

'Saartjie Baartman (more commonly known as Sarah or Sara Baartman) was born in the 1770s in the Gamtoos Valley of South Africa. In 1810, she went to England with her employer, a free black man (a Cape designation for someone of slave descent) called Hendrik Cesars, and Alexander Dunlop a Scottish doctor at the Cape slave lodge. They sought to show her for money on the London stage. Sara Baartman spent four years on stage in England and Ireland. Early on, her treatment on the Piccadilly stage caught the attention of British abolitionists, who argued that her performance was indecent and that she was being forced to perform against her will. Ultimately, the court ruled in favor of her exhibition after Dunlop produced a contract made between himself and Baartman.

'In our own century scientists have been much fascinated by "the Hottentot Venus". In the 1800s, people in London were able to pay two shillings apiece to gaze upon her body in wonder. Baartman was considered a freak of nature. For extra pay, one could even poke her with a stick or finger. Sara Baartman's organs, genitalia and buttocks were thought to be evidence of her sexual primitivism and intellectual equality with that of an orangutan. Cuvier, who had met Baartman, notes in his monograph that its subject was an intelligent woman with an excellent memory, particularly for faces. In addition to her native tongue, she spoke fluent Dutch, passable English, and a smattering of French. He describes her shoulders and back as "graceful", arms "slender", hands and feet as "charming" and "pretty". He adds she was adept at playing the Jew's harp, could dance according to the traditions of her country, and had a lively personality.'

I had scarcely finished reading this short extract and was pondering the vicissitudes of womanhood when Frank appeared in the doorway.

'Laura, I thought I should mention that Mrs Verity is taking the coach to Bath this afternoon. It is her annual visit to the spa waters. It occurred to me that, after our work is concluded, you might join me for dinner. I have an excellent Tokay I thought you might like to share.'

I felt myself turning crimson.

'That would be splendid,' I replied, my voice trembling slightly.

I spent the rest of the morning and afternoon in a state of feverish anticipation. What precisely did Frank mean by telling me that old Mrs Verity was going to Bath? And what was being suggested about dinner? I had never been with a man before and my only experience of such things had been what I had witnessed in my parents' bedroom all those years ago. I hoped that such suffering between a man and a woman was not universal. The hours before dinner seemed to drag by. Eventually I heard the grandfather clock in the hall chime the hour of six and I went down to the dining room. I was wearing a black, brocaded dress and my mother's set of pearls. Frank rose to greet me.

'Ah, there you are, Laura. I have given Tilly the night off, so we shall have to serve ourselves, I'm afraid.'

A veritable feast lay before me. There was a choice of soups, a roast lamb main course, and a mouth watering selection of desserts. In addition to this, Frank had poured us both a large glass of wine. He raised his glass to me.

'Here's to our continued association,' he said, smiling.

Oh, how after all these years, I still cherish the memory of that meal! Frank was as charming and humorous a dinner companion as I could wish for, and seemed to have a battery of jokes and stories to share with me. Time slipped away rapidly and when I glanced at the clock I learned that it was already eight o'clock.

'Now then Miss Frankland,' said Frank, with a soft lilt in his voice, 'how about another, equally delightful course - upstairs?'

I giggled at the suggestion, having consumed a considerable quantity of wine, then followed Frank upstairs. At the back of my mind I could hear a small voice saying: Laura Frankland, have you completely lost your reason? This man is your employer. Under no circumstance can you permit him to be your lover.

But I did not listen to that inner voice. Instead, I did as I was instructed. First, Frank closed the bedroom door, then asked me if I should like to remove my 'outer apparel,' to use his exact words. I stripped down until I was standing only in my underwear. Then he asked me if I might permit him to remove my knickers. I whispered in a tremulous voice that I had no objection to his proposal. This he proceeded to do, gently and slowly and with infinite care. By now I was trembling with acute excitement.

'May I touch?' he asked, quietly, his voice both serious and intimate.

'My pleasure, Mr Holness,' I replied.

Frank's warm hands started to caress, first at the base of my spine, then over my ample globes, gently but firmly, and so round and down past my fundament to my labia. My suspicions of the previous day's subject were now confirmed. Frank was passionate about *la grande derriere.*

Frank and I enjoyed a year of unrestrained joy and passion before he was taken cruelly from me. It was Frank who initiated me into the arts of love, Frank who was my dearest companion. Now he is a ghost, a vivid and precious memory. His life was cut short by outrageous and cruel actions and as a result I took up residence in Bovey Tracey, where I was to marry briefly and unhappily, then meet my nemesis - the man who I now know to be a monster - the charming, cunning and poisonous Jack Stapleton.

Chapter Ten

NEWS REPORT: THE PALL MALL GAZETTE: September 28th, 1901

The body of a young boy was discovered by a cleaner in a narrow alleyway adjacent to Dorset Street yesterday morning. He had been horribly mutilated. Inspector Lestrade of the Metropolitan Police spoke to our reporter last night and confirmed that the boy was known to them as the leader of a gang of street urchins known as 'The Baker Street Irregulars.' He was formally identified as Master 'Chavvy' O'Connor and had previously been employed as a telegraph boy. He was sixteen years old.

This is the second brutal murder of a young boy in the last fortnight, the previous victim having yet to be identified. Inspector Lestrade said: 'This is a brutal and vicious murder. There are similarities with the previous case in Dorset Sreet, especially concerning the modus operandi. I appeal to the community of Dorset Street to come forward and help us in finding the perpetrator of this foul deed. If anyone recalls seeing a tall man between thirty to forty, dressed in a black ulster and carrying a brown leather bag, possibly a Gladstone bag, in the vicinity of Dorset Street late on Tuesday last, they should inform their local police officer.' When asked if the murder of the two victims was the work of a compulsive or deranged killer like Jack The Ripper, he replied that he did not subscribe to any theory at this stage of the investigation and that the crimes were certainly not the work of the Ripper. It is understood by one of our sources that he is being assisted in his investigation by Mr Sherlock Holmes of Baker Street. Extra police officers were to be seen in the neighbourhood later this afternoon, patrolling the area.

DR WATSON'S JOURNAL: SEPTEMBER - OCTOBER, 1901

I awoke in the early hours of September the twenty seventh, unable to recall any of the events of the previous evening. I soon discovered, following a short conversation with Matron, that I was in the hospital at Princetown, where I had been brought by Frankland in the early hours of the morning. Concerned that I had not returned, he had taken a lantern out onto the moor where he had found my unconscious form. I had sustained a deep cut to the forehead when I had fallen on a rock. My attacker, who had attempted to strangle me, had possibly assumed I was dead, or perhaps had been disturbed by the approach of Frankland, and for that reason I owe him my life.

As the day wore on, my memory gradually returned, but, try as I might, I could recall very little of my attacker, apart from the fact that he was wearing an unusual perfume which I could not immediately place, and the distinct impression that he was above average height. Despite being advised by Matron that I should rest, I got dressed, signed myself out of the hospital and, catching a lift from a local farmer, was soon back at Baskerville Hall. There I found a gaunt Sir Henry, waiting for me. Beside him stood

Lucy, the newly appointed maid, neatly dressed in a blue checkered dress, white apron, white collar, and short sleeves with peaked white trim. She also appeared to be tightly corsetted, for her waist seemed to be narrower than I had last observed it, adding greater shape to her already generous bosom.

'Dr Watson, what a relief to have you back. We were worried about you. I see you have been in the wars. Come inside and Lucy will fetch us both some strong tea.'

Once ensconced in a chair by the roaring blaze, I gave Sir Henry a brief description of my recent misadventure and of Frankland's rescue mission.

'Old Frankland is a remarkable fellow,' observed Sir Henry, as Lucy poured our tea. 'Did you know that he fought in the second Afghan war?'

'I did not.'

'Oh yes, and received several medals for his bravery, fighting the fierce tribesmen out there. Of course, you yourself served.'

'And still carry the wounds of that conflict.'

'Indeed, it explains much about his combative approach to others. And his taste for the rod. You knew, I take it, that he used to beat his daughter?'

'I did. That was the reason she left him.'

'And such a pity that her husband followed the same path.'

'How long were they husband and wife?'

'Only just over a year. Of course, she couldn't get a divorce, so it left her virtually penniless. Old Sir Charles helped her, as did I. And we supported her Mission - a worthy cause. Women were not meant to be treated so

harshly and beaten, don't you agree? Unless, of course it is done for mutual pleasure.'
'Surely any sort of corporal punishment administered for sexual pleasure is questionable?'
'That depends on what sort of person you might be. For my own part, I have to admit to you that in matters of the boudoir, I have always veered towards the adventurous and experimental.'
'Quite so. And may I ask, was Laura Lyons adventurous?'
'Certainly. As much as a man could wish for. You, with your knowledge of women from three continents, will surely know what I mean. I understand from Frankland that Laura kept a diary?'
'She did.'
'I should like to see its contents, in case my name is mentioned. I don't suppose you might be able to determine its present location?'
'Holmes has it.'
'Then, perhaps when he has done with it…'
'You must ask him yourself. I have not yet read it, so I cannot tell you about its contents.'
'I must be frank with you now, doctor, lately I have been much preoccupied by this business of the family curse. I find myself often in the grip of morbid fears and vivid nightmares where I see myself transformed into a wolf.'
'I recall you telling me about it.'
'How can I describe these feelings to you? It is as if I am slowly, irrevocably, sinking into the dark. Recently, I have tried to fight off these episodes through the use of alcohol and laudanum. Neither works for me.'
'Because they are both depressants.'

'Sure they are. I have even tried out cocaine. It is an excellent stimulant, yet when the effects diminish...'
'Being a colleague of Sherlock, I can confirm that.'
'Tell me, have you ever come across toad's flesh?'
'I have not. It sounds bizarre.'
'It was recommended to me by someone as a mood enhancer. But I have also discovered it to be an excellent aphrodisiac.'
'I should exercise caution in that regard.'
'You are ever the pragmatist, Watson. Anyway, what do you intend to do now that you have recovered from your injuries?'
'To discover the identity of my assailant, of course.'
Sir Henry looked up. It was Lucy, holding a familiar brown envelope.
'What is it, Lucy?'
'Telegram for Dr Watson, sir.'
I opened it.

Watson, return London immediately. Fresh developments. Holmes.

As my cab rattled its way slowly amid the mud, slush and horse droppings of the London Streets, I was struck by the tawdriness of the capital. I had grown used to the clear skies and vivid, moonlit nights of the Devonshire moors, of its variety of birds, windswept hills and strange stone monuments, the capricious mists and verdant streams. But here I was, enveloped by the chaos and noise of the great metropolis, hemmed in by omnibuses, hansom cabs that veered in and out of the often stationary traffic, the cries of street sellers and paperboys echoing around me.

After what seemed like an eternity, my cab sped along Euston Square and so on to Baker Street, where I was given a warm reception by a worried looking Mrs Hudson.

'Dr Watson, what on earth happened to you?' she asked, taking my greatcoat from me.
'It's nothing, Martha, just a little local difficulty.'
'And I thought Devonshire was a quiet and peaceful place.'
'I can assure you that it generally is,' I said, smiling at her.
'Anyway, welcome back.'
'Thank you. Where exactly is Holmes?'
'Retired to his bedroom, sir. He came in around eleven last night and in a dreadful state. A cut lip and a blow to his head, and his clothes all creased and stained.'
'Then I shan't disturb him.'
'On the contrary, he specifically asked for me to wake him, should you arrive early. I will just go and knock on his bedroom door.'
'No need, Mrs Hudson. I am sufficiently refreshed.'
Holmes was standing in the lounge doorway. He was dressed in his old mouse coloured dressing gown. His long aquiline face was pale as chalk, his hair stood awry, his left eye had a deep purple bruise and there was a long gash to his bottom lip.
'It seems we are both the worst for wear, Watson. What have you been up to to incur such punishment?'

I explained my predicament. 'You are fortunate to have lived to tell the tale, my dear fellow. Clearly, you ignored my dictum about venturing onto the moor after dark.'

'I had no choice in the matter.'

'You could have asked Frankland to accompany you.'

'And what of your own injuries?'

'Trivial by comparison with your own. I owe these cuts and blows to three thugs who pounced on me in an alleyway behind Clay Street. Fortunately, I was able to drive them off with my single - stick or things might have been very different.'

'What were you doing there?'

Holmes smiled.

'Investigating the death of young O'Connor. Fortunately I was able to fell one of them before his two companions fled the scene. He is now in the custody of Lestrade, though he will not give his name.'

'It is a dark business,' I observed.

'And it grows darker by the minute. This time it is personal, Watson, very personal. I admit that young O'Connor's death came as a great shock to me. He would have gone far if he had been given the chance. He had a strong spirit.'

'Are you any closer to the identity of the murderer? The press seem to believe that these murders are the work of a madman, akin to Jack The Ripper.'

'They are all, as usual, wrong. But the murders were indeed by the same hand.'

'But what has this to do with the murders of Laura Lyons, Sophie Richards and the disappearance of Beryl Baskerville?'

'Oh, they are certainly connected. And there is one name that connects them. That person is...'

Holmes was interrupted by a loud knocking on our door. A flustered Mrs Hudson stood in the doorway and behind her was a tall, distinguished looking man dressed in a pinstriped suit and alpine trilby.

'I'm sorry to disturb you, Mr Holmes, but the gentleman insisted...'

'That is quite alright Mrs Hudson. The gentleman is known to me.' He extended his hand to our visitor. 'Herr Gross I believe.'

'You are taller than I expected, Mr Holmes. And I see you have been practising your prize fighting!'

Holmes laughed.

'As you can see, my colleague, Dr Watson and I have both been assaulted recently. Perhaps we are getting too old for such escapades. Could we have some tea, Mrs Hudson? Sit here, Hans, and warm yourself by our fire.' Holmes stoked the coals until they blazed. 'It is a long way from Prague and you must be weary.'

'Not as much as I expected to be, thanks to your excellent train service. It is almost as efficient as the German system.'

'The professor here is the world's leading authority on forensic science.'

'Apart from yourself, of course,' said Gross. 'I have all of Mr Holmes' monographs, Dr Watson.'

'One day, when I am not beset by murder and mayhem, I intend to devote myself to a manual of criminal investigation. It shall serve as my magnum opus.'

'And perhaps your epitaph,' said I, reaching to take the tray from Mrs Hudson.
Holmes dipped a spill into the flames and relit his pipe.
'Thank you, Watson, point noted! Hans is here to give a series of lectures in forensic science.'
'Indeed, Holmes. The Royal Society were the instigators of the idea. I am not by nature a universal tourist.'
Holmes poured the tea and offered our visitor a cheroot.
'I have urged Watson here to read your book, but his German is a little rusty. This is indeed a most fortuitous meeting,' said Holmes.
'Oh, why so?'
'I was hoping you might be of some small assistance to me.'
'In what regard?'
'No doubt you have heard of the savage cases of mutilation here in the city?'
'The two telegraph boys?'
'Yes.'
'Of course I have only read the news articles in The Times and The Globe.'
'I have here the pathologist's reports on the two victims. It makes for grim reading.' Holmes passed the files to him.
'You would like my opinion of the matter?'
'As the author of 'Kriminalpsychologie', most certainly.'
The professor, cigar lit, poured over the files as Holmes leaned back in his chair and steepled his hands in silence.
At length, he removed his gold rimmed glasses and stubbed out his cigar.
'Have you come across the work of Krafft Von Ebbing?' he asked.

'The name is familiar to me. The Austrian psychiatrist?'
'The same. His *Psychopathia Sexualis: eine Klinisch-Forensische Studie* is a landmark in the history of forensic psychiatry.'
'I confess I have not read it.'
'It has yet to be translated into English, so controversial are its studies of human perversity. Yet it is one of the most remarkable books ever written. I recommend it to you, in fact, I have a spare copy I should like to give you.'
Hans Gross reached into his attache case and brought out a plain covered book which he presented to Holmes.
'Among the many aspects of deviant sexuality it cites, the section on what Krafft Ebing calls 'Lust Murder' provides some insight into these London murders, and would equally explain the phenomenon of your 'Jack The Ripper.''
'Go on.'
'Let me read this case study to you.'
Holmes lay back in the basket chair.
'Pray proceed.'

'On the evening of May 27, 1888, an eight-year-old boy, Blasius, was playing with other children in the neighborhood of the village of St. - An unknown man came along and enticed the boy into the woods. The next day the boy's body was found in a ravine, with the abdomen slit open, an incised wound in the cardiac region, and two stab-wounds in the neck.

'Since, on May 21st, a man, answering to the description given of the murderer by the children, had attempted to treat a six-year-old girl in a similar manner, and had only accidentally been detected, it was presumed to be a case of lust-murder. It was proved that the body was found in a heap, with only the shirt and jacket on; also, that there was a long incision in the scrotum.

'Suspicion fell upon a peasant, E.; but, on confrontation with the children, it was not possible to identify him with the stranger who had enticed the boy into the woods. Besides, with the help of his sister, he proved an alibi. The untiring efforts of the officers brought new evidence to light, and finally E. confessed. He had enticed the girl into the woods, thrown her down, exposed her genitals, and was about to abuse her; but, as she had an eruption on her head, and was crying loudly, his desire cooled, and he fled. After he enticed the boy into the woods, with the pretext of showing him a bird's nest, he was taken with a desire to abuse him. Since the boy refused to take off his trousers, he did it for him; and when the boy began to cry out, he stabbed him twice in the neck. Then he made an incision, just above the pubes, in imitation of female genitals, in order to use it to satisfy his lust. But, since the body grew cold immediately, he lost his desire, and, cleaning his knife and hands near the body, he fled. When he saw the boy dead, he was filled with fear, and his limbs became weak.

'During his examination E. looked apathetically at a garland. He had acted in a state of mental weakness. He could not understand how he came to do such a thing. He must have been beside himself; for he often became senseless, so that he would almost fall down. Previous employers report that he had periods when he was devoid of thought and confused, doing no work all day, and avoiding others. His father states that E. learned with difficulty, was unskilful at work, and often so obstinate that one did not think to punish him. At such times he would not eat, and occasionally ran away and remained all day. At such times he also seemed quite lost in thought, screwed his face up, and said senseless things. When quite a boy, he still sometimes wet the bed, and often came home from school with wet or soiled clothing. He was very restless in sleep, so that no one could sleep beside him. He had never had playmates. He had never been cruel, bad, or immoral.

'His mother gave similar testimony; and further, that, in his fifth year, E. first had convulsions, and once lost the power of speech for seven days. Sometime about his seventh year he once had convulsions for forty days, and was also dropsical. Later, too, he was often seized in sleep, and he often then talked in his sleep ; and mornings, after such nights, the bed was found wet. At times it was impossible to do anything with him. Since his mother did not know whether it was due to viciousness or disease, she did not venture to punish him. Since his convulsions, in his seventh year, he had failed so in mind that he could not learn even the common prayers ; and he also became very irascible.

'He states that, for want of courage, he had never ventured to ask coitus of a woman, though in dreams such scenes exclusively passed before him. Neither in dreams nor in the waking state had he ever had perverse instincts; particularly no sadistic or contrary sexual feelings.
Too, the sight of the slaughter of animals had never interested him.

'When he enticed the girl into the woods, his desire was to satisfy his lust with her ; but how it happened that he tried such a thing with a boy, he could not explain. He thought he must have been out of his mind at that time. The night after the murder he could not sleep on account of fear; he had twice confessed already, to ease his conscience. He was only afraid of being hung.

'The opinion (Dr.Kautzner, of Graz) showed the imbecility and neurosis of the accused, and made it probable that his crime, for which he had only a general recollection, had been committed in an exceptional (prae-epileptical) state, conditioned by the neurosis. Under all circumstances, E. was considered dangerous, and probably would require commitment to an asylum for life.'

Hans Gross put down the book and took off his glasses.

'And the point is?' asked Holmes tersely.

'The point is that there is a clear psychological profile to many of these sadistic murderers, of which 'E' is a good example. The killer is frequently a loner. He has few friends as a child. He reaches puberty and discovers that not only is he detached from his fellow human beings: he is also detached from himself and from a sense of morality. He kills on impulse but cannot rationalise his actions.'

'Your analysis is interesting, although I would disagree with the idea of the 'Lust Murder.' I believe, based on the evidence I have seen, that such murders are an attempt to control the victim. The body of the victim is seen only as an object - a sexual object, as the author suggests. However, your concept of a 'profile' intrigues me, Hans. Indeed, I have reached a similar conclusion in my study of criminal history. I shall certainly study this work with interest. Thank you.'

After our visitor had left, Holmes fell into a brown study, reloaded his old brier, then lay back in his chair, bearing the countenance of a somnolent Red Indian. It occurred to me that he was no doubt exhausted by his recent experiences and was merely re-charging his batteries. After some twenty minutes had elapsed, his eyes opened and he looked directly at me.

'I have not forgotten our previous conversation, Watson.'
'Yes, you were about to give me your opinion of the identity of Laura Lyons' murderer.'
'And of the two telegraph boys. And probably, the abductor of Beryl Baskerville.'
'I have no idea who could countenance such abominable crimes.'

'Do you recall in detail the events which marked the conclusion of The Hound?'
'My memories are clear on that point.'
'You remember that we pursued Stapleton into the fog?'
'And he lost his way and was swallowed in the Great Grimpen Mire.'
'Or so we assumed.'
'What do you mean? That he is still alive? Surely, that cannot be.'
'Regrettably, he survived the ordeal. He appears to have constructed a kind of bivouac and, with the support of a confederate from Grimpen village, who supplied him with food and extra clothing, there he remained for some considerable time. But that is the very least of it. Believe me, Watson, when I tell you that his criminal enterprise extends far beyond Dartmoor or even Devonshire. You recall your recent encounter in the moorland hut?'
'How can I forget it?'
'That was the handiwork of one Stapleton's confederates - possibly Parker.'
'And you think that he and Stapleton abducted Beryl Baskerville?'
'I am sure of it. The descriptions fit.'
'What of the other murders?'
'Laura Lyons was infatuated with him. He corrupted and abused her. She has sadly paid the price.'
'But why would he kill her?'
'Because she knew too much about his past. She was a danger to him.'
'And Sophie Richards?'

'She was employed by Stapleton to seduce Sir Henry, though I am not yet sure of his motive.'
'And she too was murdered by him?'
'For what she knew and for the sheer perversity of killing her. When she had finished being an informant, he discarded her.'
'I can hardly believe it.'
'It is true, Watson. And that is only the tip of the iceberg, I am certain of it.'
'What exactly do you mean, Holmes?'
'I had persuaded myself, foolishly, that with the death of Professor Moriarty, and the arrest of many of his known associates, London had become a slightly better place. However, my recent investigations into criminal activities in the capital has proved me wrong. Since my return from the Reichenbach Falls, there has, according to Scotland Yard, been a two fold increase in prostitution - much of it being child prostitution, mark you - and a resurgence in the quantity and variety of pornography and white slavery. I have evidence to suggest that these operations can be traced to one small group of criminals. They operate what is described as the 'pyramid' system. Those who work at the street level never know of their names or even of their whereabouts. They communicate with each other using the same crew of telegraph boys who were involved in the Cleveland Street scandal, boys who have already been corrupted by older men seeking vicarious pleasure.'
'And Stapleton is a leading member of this confederacy? How do you know all this?' I asked.
'You know my methods. I have the Irregulars, who are my eyes and ears. They can slip in and out of the streets and

houses of the metropolis, unseen by the general public. They are fast, loyal and intelligent. They are familiar with the activities of many petty criminals, and can remain incognito. Chavvy O'Connor was the best of the Irregulars and now he is lost to me. I shall not forget the manner of his death. Before he died, he and a companion were getting close to discovering the whereabouts of Stapleton, but clearly they were not alert to the danger which confronted them. That is partly why I returned to London.'

'And what of Beryl Baskerville?',

'I still have no real idea of what has become of her. She might even have been sold as a white slave and shipped to the East. Anything is possible. And now that her friend and lover is dead, we are unlikely to advance on that score. Have you read Laura Lyons' journal yet?'

'I have read half of it.'

'Then I urge you to finish it, for then you will begin to understand the depth of his iniquity.'

Holmes finished his pipe, then tapped the bowl onto the mantelpiece, emptying the plugs and dottles for use the following day. Outside, the wind had risen and the darkness of Baker Street possessed an almost stygian intensity. Despite the flaming of the fire, the hiss of the gas and the glow of the oil lamps, I began to feel a cold uncertainty which, despite the consumption of a brandy, I could not shake off.

Chapter Eleven

THE JOURNAL OF LAURA LYONS, NEE FRANKLAND.
September 28th, 1901

I do not wish to dwell much upon my short marriage to Arthur Lyons. I had met him at a Christmas Ball in Tavistock where I had been spending a short holiday with an elderly aunt, Mary Frankland. I had written to her in November, shortly after the death of poor Frank. The decision of the coroner was one of an open verdict, which angered me, since I had seen the old lady in the scullery, boiling down fly papers. Frank's family doctor, a man addicted to the bottle, and approaching his eighties, had stated at the inquest that he believed Frank had died from the toxins produced by food poisoning but I am certain that it was arsenic, administered slowly in infrequent doses, which eventually killed him. I was disappointed, too, with the local constabulary, whose examination of the body was only cursory.

Arthur Lyons was, like Frank, both charming and handsome. He had recently finished a term of duty in Peshawar where he had been so long in the sun that he had turned a nut brown colour. His commission having run its full term, he was looking for both a house and a wife and declared to me that it was 'high time he settled down.'

Frank's death had a profound effect upon my emotions. There were stages of grief, anger and then a sense of detachment and bewilderment. Small wonder was it that, vulnerable as I then was, I fell for his charms, hook, line and sinker.

We were married the following June on a blazing hot day. Arthur looked immaculate in his full military dress and sporting a red rose in his jacket button hole. I wore a white lace dress which had once belonged to my mother and which I had kept in a cardboard box all through those intervening years. Several fellow officers of Arthur were present at the ceremony, dressed in their military uniforms, which made the event even more colourful. Big, strapping fellows they were, who spent a good deal of their time talking and drinking together with Arthur at the wedding reception afterwards. Every so often they would smile and wave at me, which at the time I thought was rather curious, but which later I realise should have been a warning to me.

For the first few months after we were married, all went well. Arthur was an attentive partner who soon instructed me in the finer arts of the boudoir. His athletic frame gave him a distinct advantage over other men in matters marital and I was taught several things I had not even dreamed of doing in my younger days. Then, one afternoon in late August, a close, stifling day of humidity and rain, he returned later than usual, and evidently the worse for wear.

'Where is my dinner?' he demanded of me.

'I ate earlier. You were so late in returning I threw your portion in the bin.'
'Then you shall not be disappointed to know there will be consequences.'
'What do you mean by consequences?'
'You shall see.'
So saying, he removed his jacket and shirt, placed them on a chair, then, taking me firmly by the wrist, marched me upstairs to our bedroom.
'Arthur, whatever do you mean by this?' I demanded, but he did not reply. Instead, he went to the wardrobe and took out four silk scarves.
'Now then, you harriden, remove your garments.'
Believing that Arthur had some fresh marital game to play with me, I did as he instructed.
'Now then, lie face down on the bed.'
'What do you intend?' I asked.
'You shall soon learn of my intentions,' he replied, smiling. He walked out of the room.
'Where are you going now?'
'Never you mind!'

All manner of fantasies now passed through my mind as I lay on the bed, waiting for what might occur. Previously, Arthur had initiated me into some of the many varieties of position connected to lovemaking. The one I imagined he had in mind I had found especially arousing, though at first I was not very keen on the idea. Consequently, when he returned, I gently raised my rear, expecting to be pleasured. Imagine my utter surprise and dismay, therefore, when there was a rush of air above my back, followed by intense pain in my buttocks.

'What are you doing?' I demanded of him.

'What I should have done months ago!' came the answer. 'And now that you are helpless to resist, it will give me even greater pleasure.'

So saying, I heard Arthur run to the end of the room, then back to the bed, delivering a second crack of the whip. I caught a glimpse of it out of the corner of my eye. It was a long, black leather thing with knotted flails, of the type they use in India to train elephants.

'Are you feeling it yet?' he demanded, as the scourge came down again with such force that it made my buttocks quiver from the impact.

'Two more for disobedience and that makes six of the best!' he shouted, clearly exhilarated and running again to the back of the room. There followed the sound of his running feet, then I felt a wicked blow to my left, then right cheek.

'There, we are done!' he concluded. 'Let that be a lesson to you,' and he began to release the silk scarves from my hands and feet.

'No, stay exactly where you are and I shall apply a little ointment.'

I did as I was instructed. Soon the pain was dulled to a not unpleasant ache. As Arthur gently rubbed the afflicted area, I began to experience the most delicious glow, and I almost drifted off to sleep, when I heard Arthur whisper in my ear, 'Now relax and I shall soon bring you some well earned pleasure.'

So saying, I felt his hands moving past my fundament to my moistened lips, and having worked in some more of the soothing ointment, I let out a small moan. There was a pause and I could hear Arthur removing his belt and trousers.
'You may look if you wish,' he said calmly. 'Now begins the fun!' he said excitedly and I felt the warmth of his flesh as, with one swift movement of his thighs, he entered me.

That episode marked the beginning of my initiation into the distorted world of Arthur Lyons. Such sessions took place thereafter on a regular basis, three or four times a week. Then, in the autumn of the next year, matters between us took a more disturbing direction. Arthur arrived home one evening and announced that we would be attending a 'military wives' party. Since I had not met more than a handful of women since we moved to the area of Okehampton, I welcomed this diversion, and on the Friday following, we walked along side roads to a large five - bedroomed villa on the edge of the town.

'You will remember Billy and Fred, who were at our reception?' asked Arthur.
'I do, though I did not speak to them much.'
I recalled them well, both handsome and striking men, smartly dressed in their uniforms.
'This evening was largely their idea, but I decided to fall in with their plan,' said Arthur, cheerily. 'And now we have about twenty of us from the officer's mess coming to join us.'

'How very sociable of them. I can't wait to see them all - the other wives I mean.'

'Oh we are a jolly lot and very broadminded as I hope you are, Laura. I would not have suggested this soiree otherwise.'

I was not quite sure what Arthur meant by 'broadminded,' so I did not reply.

We climbed the steps of the grand town house and the door opened, revealing an ancient retainer in a dress suit who took our coats and ushered us into a large, high ceilinged lounge, its walls decorated with rich tapestries, portraying scenes of a classical nature. These depicted satyrs chasing naked men and women through a dense forested landscape. This should have given me a clear idea of what might have followed, but I did not give it much thought.

We were welcomed by a good looking young man called Billy who brought us both a large glass of wine each and then engaged me in light conversation. After about twenty minutes had elapsed, my glass was recharged once more and Arthur and I sat down at one of the round tables next to another couple who I did not know.

'Is this your first time?' asked the woman sitting opposite, who had introduced herself as Clara.

'Yes.'

'It always excites me when I come here. One never knows quite what to expect, and that is what gives the occasion such a frisson.'

'You are intriguing me, Clara. Exactly what happens?'
'Why, did not Arthur tell you?'
I flushed.
'No, actually he did not.'
'Well, it begins with the husbands playing rounds of poker.'
'That sounds rather dull to me. What are the wives doing all this while?'
'Oh, we all get rather tipsy and excited while we wait for the results.'
'Why is that?'
'Oh, Laura, you are such an innocent! Why, of course, the man who wins each round of cards gets to choose.'
'Choose what precisely?'
'Why, one of us, you silly!'
I must confess that when I heard these words, I grew cold at the thought of what that implied.
'And you all concur with this arrangement?' I asked.
'Naturally we do. Otherwise we would not come here each Friday evening. As the number of couples has increased, the choice has become much greater. Last week, for example-' (here she lowered her head and spoke in a whisper) ' I was summoned to one of the rooms with a man whose name was Charles. A real gentleman, but altogether quite forceful, and rigid, rigid as a board when it came down to it. I spent a delightful half hour with him and only wish it had continued until dawn!'

I confess to you that this graphic utterance dismayed me. I had been brought up by Christian parents who, though not beyond reproach, considered the state of monogamy to be absolute and requisite, especially of a wife. I said nothing but merely smiled at Clara, hardly able to believe what she had just confided in me.

I did not have to wait for very long. A small chamber orchestra which had been playing now came to an end and cleared the floor. Card tables were put into place by three flunkies who then left us. The menfolk sat round the tables, chatting and smoking together, all the while drinking their whiskies and rums. At last there was a roar from the table on our left and I heard my name being called out. Blushing, I stood up and looked across the room where I saw at once that it was Arthur's friend, Billy. He strode over to my table and, smiling, said in a low voice: 'Are you ready for action, Laura?' Feeling quite bewildered by now, I nodded and my companion led me up the stairs to a large bedroom, plushly decorated in reds. There was a low, green chaise longue, a wash stand and a large bed with silk sheets. Billy pulled back the bedsheet, then turned to smile at me.
'Are you feeling nervous, Laura?'
I perched myself on the chaise longue and crossed my legs. I was glad that I had changed into a comfortable dress and discarded my whalebone corset for a more comfortable silk shift and silk cami - knickers, for that helped me relax a little.

Billy poured us each a large glass of wine.

'Here, this might help you to unwind a bit.' Then, after a short pause, he added in a quiet voice: 'I get the impression that you have never done this kind of thing before?'
'I have never heard of it.'
'It is all the rage in London, you know. They have been doing this sort of thing for years in Notting Hill and Kensington where my parents reside. It was started in America - where new ideas often spring from.'
'Have you been with many...?' I blushed at this point.
Billy took my hand and squeezed it gently.
'I have enjoyed the company of several married ladies in this way. Look, I can see you are feeling nervous. There is no need to be and you need not fret. I can assure you that I shall be gentleness itself.'
Billy looked directly at me. His eyes were an iridescent blue and quite hypnotic.
'Why should I believe you?'
'Because, dear Laura, I would not lie to a lady. I never have.'

He squeezed my hand again, this time more firmly, then moved closer to me. His hand was firm and warm.
'I am glad to hear of it.'
'As I say, you may trust me in this endeavour. Do you find it a little too warm in here?'
'I had not noticed,' I replied, squeezing his hand.
'Then you have no objection if I should remove my jacket and shirt?'
'I have no objection. This is a most sumptuous room,' I added, trying to make small conversation, though my heart

was now beating fast and the wine was making me a little light headed.

'Sumptuous indeed. The perfect setting for a little fun and pleasure, do you not agree? Have you seen these paintings by the way? They were done by a friend of Beardsley. Rather stirring I thought.'

I looked across the room at a large oil painting. It depicted the Rape of The Sabine Women. It was clearly a copy of the original by Jacques Louis David and showed several naked Roman soldiers deflowering young women. I found the depiction of the womens' plight deeply affecting.

'I find it quite disturbs me,' I replied.

Billy had now removed both jacket and shirt and his well shaped torso shone by the light the fire.

'Are you fond of photography?' he asked, starting to unbutton his trousers.

'I know next to nothing about it.'

'I should love you to sit for a studio photograph. You would make a perfect subject, Laura. I have a friend who does such things in London. A chap called Stapleton. He is especially good at putting ladies at their ease. I could introduce you to him. He is coming to visit us next weekend. I am sure Arthur would not object to such a proposal?'

'I confess I had not thought of doing such a thing, though I imagine such an experience to be pleasurable.'

'Then I shall be happy to make the arrangements.'

As he said these words, Billy removed his trousers to reveal a pair of well muscled, powerful thighs. I could not fail to notice that his underpants bore a large projection in their middle, a fact which I blush now to admit, aroused me considerably.

'You are not apprehensive now, I trust?'

'No, not - not at all,' I stuttered.

'Then let me reveal my intentions, dear Laura.'

So saying, he pulled down his pants. I found myself blushing but it was not because of any embarrassment.

'I think you might have been correct about the temperature of the room,' I replied. 'Perhaps if you turned down the gas lamps, it might help to -'

' - create an ambience. My thoughts entirely!'

He strode across the room in front of me, his shapely buttocks rippling as he went.

'And one thing more.'

'Anything, dear lady.'

'Perhaps you would be kind enough to undress me?'

'It shall be my pleasure, Laura.'

I shall never forget that evening with Billy Wright, officer and gentleman. It stays in my memory and was an experience I savour, even years later. My companion stood before me in his naked glory and began to disrobe me with infinite care and all the while looking steadily into my eyes.

First, he unbuttoned my dress, and helped me step out of it. Then he removed my silk shift, commenting admiringly on the fineness of its quality, adding: 'French, I do believe.' Kneeling before me, he then gently pulled down my black silk camiknickers whilst I helped by removing my brassiere. For some moments he continued kneeling and running his strong hands over my thighs and buttocks, so that I was left trembling with anticipation. 'May I continue, dear Laura?' he asked in a whisper. 'You must do as you please, sir,' I replied, my voice shaking. Billy buried his face in my *mons veneris*.

I shall not burden or embarrass the reader further with details of what passed between us that night. Suffice to say that by the time that Arthur and I got home in the small hours, I positively glowed. I had never before experienced such intense pleasure being with a man, not even with Arthur, who, by comparison, was a mere novice in the *arts de l'amours*. I now knew that love making was a creative thing, and not the mechanical process I had experienced with Arthur. Billy made love in ways I could never have imagined, using his strong thighs and soft hands, exploring every inch of my skin. For the rest of that night, well into the week that followed, I thought of nothing else.

It seems inevitable to me now, looking back, that I should take up Billy's kind offer to have my photograph taken in London. Arthur, though initially unresponsive to the idea, at last yielded to me. I had never been to that great metropolis before and was both excited and dismayed at what I saw as we made our way across the city in a hansom cab. Such a plethora of busy but rubbish strewn, smelly streets I had not imagined. Everywhere, it seemed, ran hordes of ragged, bare footed street urchins and many of the street sellers looked thin and weary. But there were also fine ladies, in fashionable French dresses, accompanied by prosperous, dark suited gentlemen. And everywhere the sounds of rattling, clattering conveyances, the cries of news vendors and the smells of perfumes, horse manure, sweat and soiled clothing.

Mr Stapleton's studio lay in a narrow side road between the Charing Cross Road and St Martins Road. I noticed that there were several small bookshops in this vicinity, many of them selling what Billy referred to as 'amorous fiction.' On entering the premises, we were taken upstairs by a tall negro, and found there a large room with darkened windows with two large reflector lamps, which provided illumination. There was a green chaise longue in the centre of the room, surrounded by luxurious red drapes. To my surprise, on the chaise longue lay a large, dark haired woman of middle - eastern appearance who was entirely naked except for a gold necklace and long black silk stockings.

A tall, lean man emerged from behind a bamboo screen and addressed us. Despite his slight form, he was good very looking, wore a thick waxed moustache and had penetrating dark eyes.

' Billy Wright, as I live and breathe!' he exclaimed.
'And this is Mr John Stapleton,' said Billy, 'photographer and man of many talents.'
'Known among his circle of friends as Jack,' said Stapleton.
'This is Mrs Lyons, Arthur's wife.'
Stapleton looked at me intently.

'It is a pleasure to meet you. Such fine features and delicate skin. You will do very nicely. You possess what some photographers term 'a photogenic face,' Mrs Lyons. I congratulate you. You have done exceedingly well to bring her here, Billy.' He turned and said to the model: 'Alright, you can go now. Be back here at nine sharp. We shall be doing the tableau, so do not be late!' The model disappeared behind the screen. 'Not very bright, I'm afraid, but she has just the right shape! Now, dear lady, first let us make you comfortable and relaxed. Please take off your coat. Good, good. Perch yourself here on the couch, just so, and perhaps spreading your dress thus, to reveal just a tiny glimpse of those rather fine ankles. That's perfect! And leaning back thus, yes, you have it! Perhaps unbuttoning a little of your blouse to reveal that swan like neck…And, maybe, letting down that luxuriant hair of yours? Good. I think we are almost there, Mrs Lyons, almost there. And say 'cheese' for me when I am ready to start.'

I did as I was instructed, relaxing now. There was a flash of light, a pause, then another flash. Stapleton emerged from the camera hood and smiled. 'That will do very well, I think. Now, if you would like to wait in the adjoining room, I shall be with you in a short while. There is a cabinet of drinks. Feel free to imbibe.'

And so we did as he suggested. In fact, because Stapleton had been gone for an hour, we imbibed rather too much.

'Let us take a room together, Laura, and return to Exeter on the early morning train,' said Billy.
'But what will Arthur think of me?'
'He will be quite understanding, I am sure of it. We shall just tell him that we missed the last train from Paddington.'

Thus it was agreed. Stapleton returned shortly after and joined us for a drink. He had in his hand a large framed photograph which he passed to me.

'It is a very good likeness,' I observed.
'It's wonderful,' said Billy. 'You look very relaxed.'
'As I said, you possess a fine countenance and - dare I add - an even finer figure, Mrs Lyons. I should dearly love you to visit me, perhaps when you are next in London, and perhaps you will permit me to take some more photographs. You would make a splendid model for the more sophisticated ladies' magazines!'
'She would indeed!' observed Billy. 'I can just see her now, featured in The Strand!'
'You flatter me, Billy.'
'I am utterly serious.'
'Forgive me for saying so, dear lady, but Billy here is perfectly correct!'

And so it was agreed that on the following Friday I should return with Billy and have a portfolio prepared.

We did not reach Exeter until the following afternoon and by then the skies were dull and overcast. Billy had taken the wise precaution of telegraphing my husband prior to our return, and so we were both unsurprised at seeing him waiting for us on the platform. We got into the fly, Billy wrapping a blanket round my knees, for the air was biting cold. I noticed that Arthur seemed unusually quiet, for usually he was quite a talkative fellow. The journey back to our house, through heavy showers and over rough roads, seemed interminable but Billy held my hand and kept it warm in order to comfort me. At last, we came to the stuccoed portico of our town house and went in. Arthur asked for the fire to be made up for it was a chilly day and when we had warmed ourselves, he gave each of us a strong drink.

'You enjoyed yourselves then?' asked Arthur when we had finished our whiskies.
'Positively. And not only did we enjoy ourselves, but Laura has been asked by Mr Stapleton if she will return in a week's time.'
'Really? He seems to have taken quite a shine to you,' said Arthur in a colourless, almost inaudible voice.
'Stapleton is of the view that Laura would make a first rate fashion model.'
'Is that so? Well then, you must go back to see him. Who knows what will come of this new venture, Laura.'
'Well, I don't know…' I began.
'No, I won't accept a refusal. You shall book your return ticket in the morning. And Billy, you may accompany her.'
'Very well,' I agreed, weakly.

By ten o'clock we had all become rather weary and Billy announced that it was time he was leaving. Arthur seemed tense and, with few words, ushered his friend to the door.

'Is everything alright, Arthur?' I asked tentatively after Billy had left.
'No, as a matter of fact, it is not alright,' he answered tersely.
'Then please tell me what is wrong, dear.'
'I shall do better than that. I shall show you instead. Then you will remember. Wait for me in the bedroom. I shall not be very long.' Fearing what might follow, I did as I was bid and climbed the stairs to the bedroom. Five minutes had not even passed when I heard Arthur's heavy tread on the stairs. He entered, holding a long bullwhip, which he held out to me.

'This shall be the instrument of your punishment. If you act like a whore you must be treated like a whore. Bend over, madam, but first remove your clothes!'
'But why?'
'No buts or whys. It is what you have to do. Just think of it as your act of remission.'

I removed my dress and undergarments, save for my silk cami knickers, then lay face down on the bed.
'Arthur, you must not treat me too harshly,' I urged.
'And the cami knickers, or I shall do it myself!'
I did as I was told, then waited, trembling with anxiety. Then I heard the familiar run of Arthur's feet and within seconds I felt a numbing blow across my rear which forced

me to tense my buttocks. I turned to plead with him to do no more and caught a glimpse of his sweating and determined face.
'Since you have determined to whore, you shall continue to do so and pay for it!' he bellowed as the whip cracked across my already reddened cheeks.
'I am sorry for my misdemeanour! Forgive me!'
'There shall be no exceptions. Stay exactly where you are and pay your dues.'
Another crack of the bullwhip, this time close to my fundament.
So the beating continued, until I was left bloody and raw. Arthur offered me no solace, nor soothing ointment, and I was left sobbing.

The next day I determined that I should no longer be the recipient of Arthur's sadistic treatment. I packed an overnight bag and, leaving a brief note to Arthur, explaining that I should not be returning, I walked the two miles to Billy's home through winter sludge and grime. A modest villa, situated on the outskirts of the city, The Haven was for me the fulfilment of its name. I was warmly invited in and given a glass of warm rum by Billy, whereupon I burst into tears and swooned into his arms, describing to him in graphic detail what Arthur had done to me.

'I had no idea he would stoop so low,' he said. 'I had thought he believed in free love. I was wrong. You shall stay here with Tilly and me for the next few days and I shall get Tilly to dress your wounds. She will be back soon.'

'Tilly?'

'I forgot to tell you I am a married man.'

'Will she not need to be consulted?'

'Not at all. We have a very relaxed relationship. We neither of us believe in monogamy. Tilly was for a long while a lover of Herbert Wells.'

'The famous writer?'

'The very same. And a proponent of free love himself. Tilly tells me that Wells is a dynamo in the bedroom department.'

'I would not have believed it so. He is such a small and tubby gentleman.'

'He may be small but his intellect is as large, as his appetite for the ladies.'

I sighed. I felt sore and weary and my eyes were full of tears but in my heart I knew that I would never return to Arthur on any terms.

'You have been so kind to me, Billy. I shall be forever in your debt.'

'Think nothing of it, Laura. Ah, here she is. Tilly, we have a visitor!'

Billy and his wife were two of the most generous souls I have ever had the pleasure of meeting. They were, as Billy had intimated, a most liberated couple and were fond of walking round the house completely naked. At first I was most shocked by this custom but gradually I got used to seeing them thus. As things turned out, I stayed for six months with them before I moved to Bovey Tracey and fell under the influence of a man who seemed on the surface a gentleman but, as I soon discovered, was nothing but a ruthless and determined villain.

On the Friday following my desertion of Arthur, Billy and I took the train from Exeter to Paddington. Billy determined that we should travel first class and enjoy ourselves, as an antidote to my recent ill treatment. We boarded the train and in our compartment found a tall, well dressed, distinguished looking gentleman sitting and smoking a cigar. As Billy pulled back the sliding door, the stranger stood up and addressed us.

'Hope you don't object to my smoking? Some people do.'
Billy, ever the gentleman, extended a large hand in greeting.
'No objections. I don't believe we've had the pleasure.'
'Allow me to introduce myself. I am Sir Charles Baskerville.'
Billy introduced us.
'Baskerville. That's an old name. Isn't there also a Baskerville type face?'
Sir Charles chuckled.
'Yes, I believe you are right. My ancestors came over from France with The Conqueror a long while back.'
'1066.'
'Quite, but these days we Baskervilles, few as we are, are far less war like.'
'You are diminishing in number then?'
'There are only two of us left, myself and a relative who now lives in Canada.'

'I see that you are an old soldier,' said Billy, who then told him his rank.

'Yes, I saw action in the Afghan war. My company took part in the siege of Sherpur where I lost a great number of my men.'

Billy, obviously impressed by this, continued the conversation for the major part of our journey into Paddington, so that I was able to observe our new friend in detail.

As soon as Billy had introduced me, I had felt an immediate attraction to Sir Charles. He was powerfully built, being some six feet tall and his eyes were a deep blue. As he shook my hand, I felt a strong grip and when he looked at me, I was aware of a deep, searching gaze. So help me, if I had known then as I now know how he was to meet his fate, I might have prevented it.

'It has been a pleasure to meet you, Billy and Laura. You must come and visit me at Baskerville Hall when you can. We have plenty of spare accommodation and the Moor is a sight to behold, especially in Spring. Here is my card.'

By the time we reached Charing Cross, the dark skies had cleared to reveal a deep, azure sky and the murky face of the capital I had encountered on our previous visit here a week ago was transformed. We took lunch at the Criterion, then decided to walk via Denmark Street to Stapleton's studio, dropping into Foyles bookshop on the way where I purchased one of Mr Conan Doyle's excellent collections of detective stories.

Stapleton was in fine form when we eventually arrived. We found him in the studio's office, poring over a large, leather bound book, entitled 'British Butterflies.'

'Ah, you catch me at it. The study of the lepidopterae is one of my secret vices. I soon hope to augment my collection when my sister and I move to Devon. You both live in Devon, I believe, and not far from Dartmoor?'
'Exeter, as a matter of fact. A bit of a hike from there.'
'Ah, the moor is a wonderful place, alive with fauna and flora. I have visited it often, but to live there is a different matter entirely. Now then, you must have some refreshment before we begin proceedings. What will you both have to drink?'

After we had revived ourselves, Billy explained to our host that he would have to leave us as he had to visit his solicitor's in St Martins Lane. As soon as he had departed, Stapleton plied me with a second glass of wine and sat down beside me on the chaise longue.
'We have three hours to spare before my next client arrives,' he explained, 'which is plenty of time for what we have to do.'
'And what does that consist of?'
'Why, your portrait of course. And while we are at it, dear lady, what about some extra photos for your gentleman friend?'
'What had you in mind exactly?'
'I was thinking along the lines of something rather French, something a little risque.'

'Let us see how things develop,' I replied, feeling a little sleepy after the wine.

Stapleton immediately set to work, arranging the lights and encouraging me to sit thus and arrange my legs so, and to let down my long tresses, for surely he had never seen such a fine head of hair. And this was all achieved by his charm and my own compliance, for I felt pleased by his constant flattery. At last he was ready and, disappearing under the lens cloth, took the photograph.

After a little while in the darkroom, he emerged bearing the plate and showed it to me.
'Magnificent, isn't it? See how the camera has picked out your skin tones. It has almost, but not quite, done you justice, Laura.'

There was a pause, and he looked pensively at me.
'What is the matter?'
'No, it would be quite impertinent of me.'
'Nonsense. Say what you had in mind.'
'I should like to take a few more photographs of you.'
'I shall be pleased if you did so.'
'Perhaps of a more intimate nature?'
'You mean you would like it if I removed my clothes?'
'Yes, to be blunt.'
'It shall be my pleasure,' I replied, feeling unaccountably aroused. I could feel a strong magnetism towards this man with his dark hair, luxuriant moustache and hypnotic eyes. Little did I know at this juncture what lay ahead of me.

'Then let us begin. They shall be a pleasant surprise for Billy when he finally returns.'

Thus began my long and disastrous relationship with John Stapleton, who preferred to be known as Jack, John Stapleton, the photographer and lepidopterist, who masqueraded as a teacher under the alias of Mr Vandeleur, who cruelly beat his wife and who used me and abused me. Under his influence, I caused the death of Sir Charles Baskerville, who had shown me nothing but love, kindness and generosity. I thought he had perished in the shifting waters of the great Grimpen Mire, but it was not to be. Like a revenant, he emerged from that dark world to wreak havoc upon me and all who fell under his malign and poisonous influence and, just as before, I found myself powerless to resist him.

Chapter 12

DR WATSON'S DIARY, 30th October, 1901

I had seen nothing of Sherlock's brother Mycroft since the late summer, for, as he explained to us in our sitting room at 221B, he had been much preoccupied with important affairs of the State regarding the recent events in South Africa regarding the Boer War. He seemed to have aged since I last saw him and lacked his usually neat sartorial appearance. There was a sprinkling of dandruff on the collar of his suit jacket and his shoes were scuffed and unpolished. He spoke in the usual, direct and deliberate way which was his wont when addressing Sherlock, but I detected in his voice a note of world weariness.

'I thought I should come over to see you immediately about the matter,' he said, leaning forward in his chair to warm his reddened hands by our blazing fire. 'It's about the Moriarty gang. I believe you have recently had some dealings with them?'
'And continue to do so,' replied Sherlock.
'The Home Office has recently been in touch with us at the Foreign Office regarding the activities of the Fenians. You will no doubt recall the outrages in 1885 when three bombs exploded in London, in the House of Commons chamber, in Westminster Hall and in the Banqueting Room of the Tower of London. Two police officers and four civilians were injured at the time. Two men were sentenced to penal servitude for life as a result. There was

also the attempt to blow up the monarch four years ago, during the Jubilee celebrations. Since that time they have suspended their terrorist operations in the metropolis. However, Special Branch have not been idle in the interim. In fact, a squad of six officers have been working under cover constantly since the last of these outrages and they have garnered much information about their links to British criminal gangs. One of these, the so called 'Moriarty Gang,' have been setting up trade links with the Fenian Brotherhood in recent months and enabling them to purchase light and heavy duty ordnance through the ports. These weapons include gatling guns, large quantities of dynamite, rifles, hand guns and several cases of Hans rifle grenades, the latter being a recent and most devastating innovation.'

'I was not aware of the extent of this trade,' observed Sherlock, drawing on his cherrywood. 'I have been preoccupied with other aspects of the gang's operations.'

'You are referring to the telegraph boy murders?'

'Not just the murders. The majority of brothels operating here in the capital are under the control of the Moriarty gang.'

'I was not aware of it. It is not part of my remit.'

'They are also the driving power behind the pornography industry, which they have invested in heavily. At this moment they own no less than fifty small bookshops selling printed and pictorial material. They have also been responsible for the enslavement and sexual abuse of countless numbers of children under the age of fifteen.'

'Sherlock, much as I admire your concern as a social campaigner, I repeat that this is not part of my remit. You are familiar with a criminal who goes under the alias of Mr Vandeleur?'

'Jack Stapleton.'

'The same. Apparently it was thought he had died in Devonshire some while ago.'

'But that was not the case,' observed Sherlock.

'Quite. Well, it appears, from the intelligence we have compiled, that this fellow Stapleton, in collaboration with two Fenians, will attempt to kill the King at one of his official public appointments.'

'Which one?' I asked.

'That is part of the problem we are facing. King Edward has two public appointments. On Thursday coming, he addresses the British Archaeological Society in Hammersmith, and on the Friday he will give a brief address to the Royal Society at Carlton House. Naturally there will be police officers in plain clothes at each of these events, but we do not know whether there has been mechanism already set in place. There has been some intelligence in the last two weeks of a new type of bomb which uses a remotely controlled timing device, but we know little about it. So, all in all, Sherlock, I am at my wits' end to know what to do next.'

'You may leave the matter in my hands, Mycroft. I shall employ my own team to carry out a reconnaissance of both premises prior to the events.'

'Your team?'

'I refer, of course, to the Irregulars. They are my eyes and ears, and they are both diligent and invisible in their methods.'

'A collection of street urchins? Surely not, my dear Sherlock.'

'You may refer to them in that deprecating way, naturally. However, the fact remains that they have been of great service already in this vexing affair.'

'Very well, I shall leave the matter to you then.'

'Excellent. Would you join us in a glass of scotch before you go?'

Mycroft pulled out his fob watch and glanced briefly at the face.

'I'm afraid that I must be on my way, gentleman. I have a meeting with an official from the Turkish embassy.'

'Then I shall ask Mrs Hudson to call you a cab. Incidentally, Watson and I will be attending the lecture at Carlton House on Friday.'

I raised my eyebrows in mild surprise.

'Dr Gross' talk on criminological innovations, Watson. I did mention it to you some while ago.'

'Oh yes. It slipped my mind.'

'I am only sorry I shall not be there to hear it. I have much regard for the man. He and Dr Krafft Ebbing are changing the face of forensic science.'

'Indeed they are,' replied Sherlock. 'Ah, there you are, Mrs Hudson, a cab for brother Mycroft, if you would.'

Mrs Hudson dutifully obliged and Sherlock and I were left sharing the now smouldering fire. Holmes seemed more pensive than usual and sat in his chair, tapping his fingers.

'You are not entirely happy with the arrangements, I gather?'

'The arrangements are entirely adequate, Watson. No, it is not that which concerns me.'

'What is it then?'

'The sheer cunning of the man, that is what troubles me. Throughout this whole affair, he has stayed ahead of me. He mocks me, Watson, he mocks me.'

'As did Professor Moriarty, I recall. But you were the worthier opponent.'

'He is not at all like Moriarty. The Professor possessed a keen, cold intellect. He may have qualified as a megalomaniac but he was not a sadistic killer. No, Stapleton is in an altogether different league, a league of his own. In all my years as a criminal investigator, I have never come across such an individual. He is remorseless and tireless, cruel and inhuman. I knew it before and I know it now. What I did not know, however, is the extent of his network and the sheer number of his accomplices. I fear that it will take all the resources of the Metropolitan police and my own efforts to bring him and his cronies to justice. Drink up, Watson. We have much to accomplish before Friday.'

LAURA LYONS' JOURNAL, September 30th, 1901

Jack Stapleton. How the very sound of that name now fills me with loathing and dread! Yet, when I first encountered him at his studio in London, my opinion of him was entirely different. He had learned to cloak his perverse nature entirely with a facade of charm. He has a rare talent, the ability to persuade those more vulnerable than himself to obey his every whim. I have already described him briefly as having dark hair and unusual eyes. But there was something about his manner and even his way of moving which had a marked effect on women. You might call it charisma but you would be mistaken if you did. It can only be described as a kind of animal magnetism, a chemical effusion which caused an instant arousal to the recipient of his charms.

I have already outlined what occurred in Stapleton's studio on that chilly September afternoon. But what I have not described is how, even on that first rendezvous, I felt compelled to follow his instruction. Now, when I look back on that early period of our association, I can hardly believe I did those things; how I posed provocatively on the couch for him, wearing nothing but a feather boa, how I then let him dress me as a house maid, then insisted that I beat him soundly on the buttocks before making passionate love to him. There was much else besides which now makes me blush to recall and which I shall not, for common decency, set down in these pages.

When Billy finally returned late that same afternoon, I had dressed and revived my makeup, hoping that he would find nothing amiss. But I was mistaken, for Billy was more observant than I had anticipated.
'You have had relations with Stapleton this afternoon, Laura,' he stated after we had taken our seats on the train at Paddington.
'How do you know?'

'There is a hectic blush to your cheeks which makeup cannot hide.'

'You are very observant. Perhaps too observant. You do not object, surely?'

'What you choose to do, Laura, and who you choose to be with, is no one else's concern but your own. But I think I should warn you that, charming though he is, Stapleton is quite the Lothario.'

'He is promiscuous?'

'Utterly. He is also a hedonist. Always has been. Even when we were at Eton together, he was the same. I was two years his junior, of course, a mere 'fresher.' But there were several stories about him which circulated amongst us juniors or 'wets' as we were described. For example, it was believed that he hired a room at the local public house which he visited every Friday. There he hired two local prostitutes to entertain him. This arrangement was only terminated after the headmaster found out about it. The boy who snitched on him was found in a small room next to the caretaker's office the following morning. He had been so soundly thrashed that it took him two months to recover.'

'He is capable of violence, then?'

'Entirely.'

'I cannot honestly believe that.'

'Perhaps you do not believe it because he has clouded your vision?'

'How dare you say that!'

For the remainder of that long journey we sat in silence together, only speaking again when the green, rolling hills of Devonshire finally came into view.

'Diana and I are having one of our special evenings tonight by the way, should you like to join us,' said Billy.

This was a somewhat cryptic reference to Billy and Diana's 'soirees,' which was a polite euphemism for what was actually naked frolicking. I had been witness to this event shortly after I had moved in with them the previous year. Initially I had been quite shocked at what had taken place in that comfortable suburban living room with its shuttered blinds, but had slowly grown to accept the eccentric behaviour of Billy and Diana, chiefly because of their great kindness towards me. When at last I was invited to the third such occasion, I accepted, partly out of a perverse form of curiosity. For some while that evening I had sat in the basket chair, merely observing their couplings. But after a while Billy asked me in that quiet way of his if I should like to participate. I considered it churlish to dissemble and found myself pleasantly surprised at the way the rest of that evening unfolded. I must admit that my participation in these arrangements was partly due to Billy's gentle manner and his impressive physique.

'I shall look forward to it,' I replied, my manner now more compliant.

'These things I have told you about Jack. It would be well if you took heed.'

'I shall.'

But unwisely I did not heed Billy's advice about Jack Stapleton.

In the January of 1888 I was given an opportunity to improve my situation. I received a letter from my solicitor in Okehampton, asking if I might see him on a matter of some importance. Curious as to what this might be, I took the train from Exeter and walked down narrow streets to the offices of Bushthorne and Chater.
'Thanks for your swift reply,' said Mr Chater, an elderly man with white hair and pincenez glasses. I think you will be pleased with what I have to tell you.'
'What on earth is it?'
'An anonymous benefactor has provided you with a gift of a not inconsiderable sum.'
I raised my eyebrows in surprise.
'How extraordinary!'
'Yes, I thought you might be pleased to hear the good news. I shall be very pleased to write you a cheque for £20,000.'
Astonished by the news, I sat back in my chair and gasped in utter astonishment at the size of the sum.
'Who on earth might he be?'
'I am sorry, Laura, but I am not allowed to reveal the identity of your benefactor. That is part of the arrangement.'

I sat in the train compartment on my return to Exeter, still shocked at the news. Armed with this sum, I would be able to set up a secretarial agency and perhaps buy a comfortable cottage near to the city. Beryl and Diana gave me their blessing and I set about making a new life for myself.

For some months after I received this news, I tried to figure out who my benefactor might be. Eventually, I came to the conclusion that it was my dearest Billy, for he was undoubtedly one of the most generous people I have ever met. How wrong I was.

Shortly after I moved into my new abode in Bovey Tracey, I received a letter from Sir Charles Baskerville. He had seen my advertisement in The Western Morning News, offering a discreet secretarial service and he had remembered our chance meeting on the train to London. I immediately responded and he invited me to Baskerville Hall. There he confided in me that he had a number of female correspondents who frequently wrote to him 'on matters of a delicate and intimate nature.' He wished to use my address as a recipient of their letters and packages, thus maintaining complete privacy. I was only too happy to oblige and he provided me with a generous monthly sum.

It was about a fortnight after this that I encountered Stapleton. He was standing in the queue at Bovey Tracey post office, looking as suave as ever. On seeing me, he left the queue and joined me.

'What a pleasant coincidence!' he exclaimed, pressing my hand warmly. 'What brings you to Devonshire?'

When I told him of my mysterious benefactor, Stapleton gave me one of his warm, endearing smiles.
'It seems you have a guardian angel, dear lady. Are you still in contact with Billy and Diana?'
'We meet occasionally - though my work keeps me rather busy.'
'And you - are you well?'
'I am.'
'That is very good to hear. But you must surely allow time for yourself.'
'I would, if I knew more people.'
'Then you must meet my sister, Beryl - and come to one of our special evenings. I insist upon it!'
'Where are you living presently?'
'We have taken a little place right up on the Moor. It is plain and simple but the wildlife that surrounds it is something to behold. I must also introduce you to Sir Charles Baskerville. It is he who organises our little entertainments up at the Hall.'
'I know him. He is a client of mine.'
'Excellent! I can see you are already moving in the best circles.'

So it was that I was unwittingly drawn into Stapleton's dark world of crime and perversity. And once I was trapped in his butterfly net, I found it impossible to escape.

I heard nothing more of Stapleton for the next month and had almost forgotten the invitation to one of his 'soirees,' when I received a small envelope through the post, the address written in a neat copperplate hand. When I opened it there was a card which read: 'You are cordially invited to attend a masked Dionysian Evening at Baskerville Hall. This is a discreet, private event for those of a liberal persuasion. Couples and singles all welcome. Please dress accordingly. Strict anonymity confirmed. Use the east wing entrance. Starts 7.30pm, February 6th.'

I was curious about this missive, but knowing Sir Charles to be an upstanding member of the community, a benefactor, and a local magistrate, I saw this as a good opportunity to widen my social circle and quite possibly to augment my business contacts. On a chilly February evening, therefore, I took a cab from Bovey Tracey. It seemed we had been travelling for an eternity along narrow, bumpy roads but when I saw the tall chimneys of the Hall lit up by its Edison lamps, looking ghostly in moorland mist, I knew that we had reached our destination.

The east wing was some way from the main entrance to a very substantial Gothic mansion and I at once realised that Sir Charles was a man of substantial means. Having paid my fare and instructed my cabbie to return no later than eleven thirty, I pulled the door bell and was ushered inside by an elderly servant in a smart suit who introduced himself as 'Barrymore.'
'You will find the company upstairs, madam. First door on the right. May I take your coat?'
Taking my coat, he gave me a mask, decorated with black lace.

'I am instructed to tell you that you will also require this, madam.'

I climbed the stairs, stopping every so often to admire the plush, embossed red wallpaper and a series of paintings. Some of these were originals, some landscapes showing the beauty of the moors, and others which were more familiar to me and by notable artists. Among those I recognised were Manet's delicate portrait of a slave girl, Fragonard's exquisite 'The Swing,' Rubens' copy of Michaelangelo's 'Leda And The Swan,' and the delectable 'Venus of Urbino,' by Titian. All of these paintings I had regarded as profoundly erotic works and it was a pleasure to view them even though they were copies.

As I entered the room, I was at once assailed by a smell I had first encountered on a holiday I spent with my parents in Egypt many years ago. It was undoubtedly hashish. 'Welcome, Laura. I was so pleased you could attend our little gathering,' said a beaming Sir Charles as he took my hand. 'Do allow me the pleasure of introducing you to some of our participants. First names only, as I am sure you are aware!'

I surveyed the room, which had been painted in the classical Italian style. Heavy, red curtains covered the long Gothic windows, whilst the room was furnished with a series of ornate divans and sumptuous velvet cushions. Upon these cushions sat a collection of men and women, all wearing masks similar to my own. Some of the company were smoking hashish from what I believe is termed a 'bubbler,' or a device consisting of a bong and a pipe, used to cool the smoke.

I also could not help but notice that many of the women were quite scantily dressed. Some wore a white toga, of the type associated with ancient Rome. Many of the men also wore the togas, except for a few who wore virtually nothing save a thong, a pair of open toed sandals and a floral headpiece.

I soon fell into conversation with a group of ladies who were sitting near the entrance at one of the small round tables. They introduced themselves as Diana and Gloria, and seemed used to the proceedings. Diana, the older of the two, was a large framed woman, clad in a white silk dress with a deep plunge at the chest, revealing her large breasts. Her shorter companion was wearing a short, classical tunic made of thin, see through muslin. It was pulled in tightly at the waist, emphasising her ample thighs.

'Is this your first time?' Diana asked me.
'Yes.'
'Gloria and I have been to several of these little soirees. At first we found it all rather daunting, didn't we Gloria?'
'But we hadn't realised exactly what was involved.'
'No, we hadn't. Then, after that first evening, we could not wait until the next one.'
'That's right. Of course, the mask is the thing that helps everyone. It liberates you.'

'It certainly does,' concurred Diana. 'And of course, using only our first names. What a delightful dress you are wearing, Laura. French silk, isn't it? I love those bare shoulders and pagoda sleeves! And that simply exquisite amber necklace.'
'Thank you. But I must ask: what exactly happens here?'
'Why, did not Sir Charles or Mr Stapleton explain it to you?'
'They did not explain.'
'Then no wonder you look rather confused, poor dear. It's very simple, really. The gentlemen first decide who they most prefer and then they come round the tables and select them,' said Diana, refilling my glass with wine.
'Sometimes a gentleman may choose more than one lady,' added Gloria. 'That can be *very* stimulating.'
'Twice that has happened - to both of us!' Diana smiled at her companion knowingly.
'Sometimes, there will be someone else who just likes to stand and watch.'
'Yes, at first I found that a little distracting, but after a short while I found that it heightened the pleasure.'
'And then, on some occasions, Mr Stapleton likes to take photographs, which he gives us copies of, should we desire them. Are you acquainted with Jack and his sister Beryl? I think that they are sitting over there.'

For the sake of common decency, I shall not dwell too much on the further events which took place at Baskerville Hall on that winter evening. The rooms allocated for these incognito liaisons were delightfully furnished in what I believe is called the 'Art Nouveau' fashion and the beds were large and comfortable, each having a large mirror mounted in the ceiling, thus adding to the overall effect of what occurred beneath. I shall be frank here in saying that, although I had thought myself to be broad - minded, I was to learn from those evening soirees much that challenged and stimulated me. I became, as I believe the fashionable phrase goes, 'a new woman,' - until, that is, I fell under Stapleton's spell and went down into the dark.

It was just after this episode that Stapleton introduced me to Beryl. At first I imagined she was Jack's sister, for she was introduced to me as such. Only later did I discover that actually they were man and wife, indeed, had been for many years. She had met him whilst he had been on a visit to Costa Rica in order to study and collect a number of rare butterflies which flourish there. She told me that she at once fell under his spell and married within the month. She had been drawn to Stapleton because of what she referred to as his 'splendid physique' and his tales of his exploits in India during the Afghan War. At first he had been a gentle and considerate husband, but as time went on, Beryl began to see another side to this well mannered Englishman. He began demanding that they should make love *al fresco*, often choosing locations such as forest footpaths or narrow alleyways where there was a strong risk of being seen by members of the public. He told her that such acts added to their excitement. Beryl complied with these requests, though with some reluctance.

After they arrived back in England, Stapleton managed to secure funds in order to open a boys' preparatory school,

Beryl assisting him as a matron. Beryl told me that Stapleton had received a large sum of money from his father, who had died in South America. They had assumed the name of Vandeleur in order to conceal Stapleton's true identity because, when they had been in Costa Rica, Stapleton had got into a fight with two men who had accused him of being a pansy. Stapleton retaliated angrily. One man was knifed in the heart and his companion received a severe beating. A witness to this attack described Stapleton as 'looking like a man possessed by demons.' The couple then left Costa Rica and arrived back at Portsmouth several weeks later, virtually penniless.

All did not go well at the school in Whitby. Stapleton had developed a taste for beating boys in his office, using a riding crop These were boys who had committed some minor misdemeanour. Some of the staff at the school took exception to the length and severity of these beatings, noting that one of the sessions lasted half an hour and the pupil concerned had to be hospitalised. The school ran at a severe financial loss and its fate was subsequently sealed when there was an outbreak of influenza and three pupils died as a result.

Faced by financial ruin, the two travelled to London where Jack met up with several of what he described to Beryl as 'old business associates.' He then gained employment at an office in London. Stapleton appeared to prosper and they moved to a spacious house in Lewisham where Jack used the railway to commute to his work. He told Beryl little about the precise nature of his activities, save that it was in the photographic line. About a year later, he announced to his wife that they were moving to the west country so that he might continue to expand his photographic affairs. And so they had come to the place on the Moor. It was Stapleton who introduced me to Beryl that fateful evening at one of Sir Charles' 'soirees,' and it was then that I fell instantly in love with the woman who was to be both my inspiration and my eventual nemesis.

Chapter 13

DOCTOR WATSON'S DIARY, 15th November, 1901

The day that is forever etched in my memory dawned sunny and cloudless, and without even a hint of the dreadful events which would follow on that fatal Friday. For once, Holmes was punctual to breakfast, having washed and shaved ahead of me, and I found him sitting at our breakfast table, humming a tune from a Verdi opera.

'Nabucco, I believe?'
'Rigoleto. Clearly my delivery was inexact, Watson. But it is, nevertheless, a very good morning.'
'You are in a positive mood today.'
'I have some reason to be so.'
'How so?'
'Because my investigation is proceeding with vigour, thanks mainly, I must say, to my informants in the underworld.'
'And the Irregulars.'
'Quite so. They have been invaluable. I now have a considerable sum of evidence to indict Mr Jack Stapleton. What I lack, however, is his present whereabouts.'
'But he is here in London?'
'Oh undoubtedly. However, his web of infamy still extends as far west as Devonshire.'
'And how will you sever that network?'
'By first eliminating the spider at the centre of the web.'

'Have you any idea yet as to Beryl Baskerville's whereabouts?'

'I believe he is keeping her prisoner, most likely at his present location. For what dark reason I cannot quite yet determine. He is cunning, Watson, oh, so cunning, and that is why the foxhound must reach his prey sooner rather than later. While he lives, he is a threat to many of us, but especially to Sir Henry and his wife. Now, finish your kippers, my dear fellow and I shall call a cab to take us to Carlton House. The police and the Irregulars have thoroughly swept the area for suspicious objects, so we can enjoy the proceedings.'

Sadly, however, our afternoon at Carlton was to be short lived.

Our cabbie took us on a circuitous journey through the back streets of SW1, via Cork Street, Duke Street, then on to prestigious Pall Mall. I was reminded of how poverty and neglect blighted the capital, for I observed many ragged clothed children on our route. Some of them looked as if they had not eaten for weeks. Their scarred, pock marked faces and watery eyes showed the state of dire poverty and utter helplessness that had prematurely aged them. Some even carried pale faced, mewling infants strapped to their backs. It occurred to me then, that despite the greatness of our Empire, we had done very little to rid ourselves of the plague of poverty and that these were precisely the sort of wretched individuals who were subject to Stapleton's demonic machinations.

As we turned the corner of Carlton Terrace, Holmes leaned forwards, frowning.

'Do you smell it, Watson, can you see it?' he shouted.

I leaned forwards and immediately saw the blazing inferno that was once Carlton House. Smoke and flames billowed from its upper windows and had already reached the roof. The grand stucco pillars which had once adorned the front porch of the building had completely gone and the oak doors lay some distance from the entrance as if some giant figure had burst his way out, leaving a scene of utter destruction in his wake.

Several bloodied figures staggered into the road, almost colliding with our hansom cab and would have died under its wheels had our driver not been so astute. I saw one man who had lost his arms entirely and lurched from the scarred opening of the house with blackened face, blood pumping from his shattered stumps. A woman who followed him out, her dress in tatters from the blast, her face shattered by metal fragments, fell onto the bloody pavement, then convulsed and instantly expired. I had not seen such an atrocity since my days in Afghanistan.

'Wait here, Cabbie,' Holmes ordered, his face ashen, 'we may be some time.'

Through the belching, acrid smoke we glimpsed fire engines attempting to extinguish the fierce blaze and the blue uniforms of several police officers, many offering

first aid to the victims. One of the officers instantly recognised Holmes and stepped forwards to speak.
'Mr Holmes?'
I'm Sergeant Wilkes. Detective Chief Inspector Lestrade asked if he could have a word, sir.'
'Lead the way then. Watson, you may wish to stay here.'
'I shall. I only wish to God I had brought with me my medical bag.'

For what seemed like hours, I administered what little help I could offer the poor, mutilated wretches who I tried to assist, but often my medical knowledge was of limited use to them and they slipped into a coma or passed away in my arms. One poor man, who had lost one of his arms and both legs below the knees, asked me in his last dying moments why God should permit such things, and I could not answer him.

At last, when the last of the casualties had been taken away in ambulances, Holmes emerged from the ruins of the building, his face set and grim, his clothes stained with ash and soot.
'What did Lestrade have to say?' I asked, tentatively, wiping the blood from my hands.
'It is a very bad business. Twenty dead, thirty four with serious injuries. Thank God that the King himself had just left the building when the first of the bombs was detonated.'
'There was more than one bomb?'

'There were two bombs, both of which were worn under the coats of the assailants. One was detonated, then the other, a few seconds afterwards.'

'And their bodies?'

'It would take a pathologist many hours to piece together the fragments of muscle and bone. I warn you, it is like a slaughter house inside.'

'I have no intention of going inside, I can assure you.'

'Forgive me, Watson. I should have thought. You are no doubt exhausted. What I can tell you, however, is that the men responsible for this heinous crime were undoubtedly Fenians. A label attached to the inside of one of their greatcoats taught me as much. It bore the legend of 'Doyle and Leckie, Gentlemens' Outfitters, Dublin.''

'What of our German friend?'

'Dr Gross? Thankfully, he survived and received only slight injuries to the arms and face. He has been taken to Saint Thomas' Hospital.'

'But how on earth could this happen?'

'Despite the elaborate precautions taken, they outwitted us. Lestrade believes the two men had taken the role of security officers and had gained entrance through a back door to the building. Once in, they just had to position themselves, one near the stage, the other at the back of the hall. Fortunately, both His Majesty and Dr Gross had just exited by one of the side entrances, accompanied by two Special Branch officers. However, none of this will be much consolation to the victims' families. I take full responsibility for what has taken place here, Watson. I simply did not anticipate the possibility of a human bomb.

It seems that, once more, Stapleton has remained one step ahead of us.'

It was a relief to both of us when at last we reached the comforting sitting room at 221B. The intrepid Mrs Hudson insisted on taking both our greatcoats and Holmes was too weary to resist. Reaching for the gasogene and tantalus, he poured us both a large measure of scotch and we sank, exhausted, into the two basket chairs while Mrs Hudson prepared supper for us. Holmes reached for his old clay pipe and, plugging it with a large handful of shag, leaned back in his chair, blowing smoke rings into the air. He looked completely exhausted.

After a few minutes, Mrs Hudson re-appeared bearing a large tray with two plates of cold meat salads. Holmes roused himself from his reverie and began to devour the meal.
'So - what now?' I queried.
'We wait, Watson, and we watch. Sooner or later, the rat will emerge from its lair. Then we shall be ready for him. And not just Stapleton, either. We shall also lay our hands on his compatriots, the individuals responsible for the abduction and abuse of countless women and children, and a vast empire of pornography.'

No sooner had Holmes uttered these words than our landlady appeared at our sitting room door.
'Thank you, Mrs Hudson. It was an excellent meal.'
'Wiggins, sir. He's waiting to see you.'
'Ask him to come up.'

I had not seen Wiggins of the Irregulars for some while and had forgotten how tall and lean he was. He had aged slightly and filled out around his arms and shoulders but still had the alert manner and quick, darting face which I recalled from before. He was wearing the uniform of a telegraph boy with smart jacket and trousers and peaked cap.

'Well Wiggins, what have you got for me?'

'The business, Mr 'olmes. We found out where Stapleton was hid.'

'*Had* been hiding,' Holmes corrected him. 'Where is he hiding?'

'A place just off Goulston Street.'

'Whitechapel,' Holmes mused. 'Curious, Watson. Goulston Street was one of the Ripper's old haunts.'

'A coincidence?'

'I am not certain of it. I would not altogether discount it. Well done, Wiggins. The Irregulars have certainly lived up to my expectations. Now, I want you to do one further thing for me. I shall you a cab, and you shall go directly to Scotland Yard. Ask for Inspector Lestrade. Tell him what you have told me and ask him to meet us here at five o'clock this evening. Tell him to come armed.'

'Is that ev'rything, Mr 'olmes?'

'That is all.'

By the time we reached Whitechapel, it was already dark and the drizzling rain and gas-lit streets gave me a feeling of intense melancholy. I had contacted Rachael soon after my return to London, only to discover that she had acquired a new gentleman friend, a portly, red faced, rather shabby genteel fellow in his sixties, who doffed his hat to me upon my arrival at her flat. When I enquired of her as to his identity and character, she answered that he was a client, nothing more. On receiving this news, my heart sank. I realised that nothing could be gained from continuing our relationship for much longer. We ate dinner together and, after a brief bout of love making, I left and caught a cab back to Baker Street, convinced that I should write to her and explain my feelings.

I had forgotten how tawdry and unsavoury the area was, with its narrow, cheap tenements, each crowded with down trodden families, pickpockets, palmers, knobblers, punishers and all manner of malcontents. Our route took us down Chicksand Street, then a narrow alleyway behind Montague Street for what seemed like an eternity. Everywhere we walked there was a sour odour, comprising stale cabbage, dog faeces, coal smoke and urine. Occasionally, figures would loom out of the shadow to us, revealing a raggedy clothed ne'er do well, a bottle of cheap gin in his hand, mumbling incoherently. At such moments, Holmes would raise his silver knobbed singlestick at them and they would scuttle back into the dark.

Eventually, we arrived at our destination, a row of narrow, yellow bricked housing, each house showing signs of wear with rotting, paint peeled window frames and doors. Drifting through the cold night air came the sounds of dogs barking, children wailing and adult voices raised in anger. The feeling of melancholy which had dogged me earlier now gave way to despair. I felt as if I were a bystander in one of Heironymous Bosch's depictions of Hell.

'Here it is,' Holmes whispered to Lestrade. 'Number 26, Goulston Street.'

The place lay cloaked in darkness. Lestrade crouched down and lit his dark lantern.
'See that you have your revolver ready,' Holmes instructed me. I reached into my greatcoat pocket and feeling the cold steel of the barrel drew it out and removed the safety catch.
'I am ready, Holmes.'
'Then let us proceed with extreme caution.'
'I will take the back entrance,' Lestrade said softly. 'Mr Holmes, Doctor, the front entrance. Any problems, just use this police whistle. I have four plain clothes officers down the street.'

Holmes took a burgling pick from the inside of his coat and jiggled it back and forth inside the mortice lock until there was a sudden snap and the door creaked open. For a few seconds we both stood in silence, waiting to see if we had been detected. Then Holmes motioned me forwards along the darkened hallway. The ground floor lay in almost pitch darkness but the bright light of a newly risen moon and the guttering street light provided a little illumination as we paced along the hall, then began mounting the threadbare stairs. There was a smell of disuse and decay about the place, mixed with the familiar odour of oil lamps.

We reached the landing, where Holmes bade me stop. Slowly, he turned the door handle of the main bedroom, then pushed the door wide open. But the room was empty save for a rusting bedstead, a small bamboo table and a stinking, unemptied chamber pot. We moved back across the landing where moonlight streamed through a cracked window. Again, the room was sparsely furnished, but this time we were luckier. A stout oak chair stood next to a single bed whose cover and sheet had been thrown back, suggesting that someone had recently been here.

'Our bird has flown, Watson. We are just too late. Ah, inspector, any luck?'
'It's as quiet as a churchyard. We seem to have missed the boat.'
'So it appears.'
'Nonetheless, you may find the cellar of some interest, Mr Holmes.'
'Lead the way then.'

A large trapdoor led us down uneven stone steps to the cellar where Lestrade opened the shutter on his lantern and moved the light slowly around the damp walls. In the middle of the room stood a large oak bench. On it were strewn a medley of assorted weapons, whips, bludgeons, chains, handcuffs and cloth restraints, including a strait jacket. A long backed wooden chair stood by the bench and on its arms there lay two steel restraining cuffs. Holmes knelt down and smelled the arms and back of the chair.

'It is blood. And in copious amounts. I do believe this has been Stapleton's torture chamber.'

'And over here, Mr Holmes,' said Lestrade, pointing to a corner of the room and shining his lantern on a pile of clothing. Holmes picked up a woman's dress, a black brassiere and a crumpled pair of cami - knickers. He smelt the dress.

'Beryl Baskerville. The perfume is quite unique. French, originating from a small perfumery near Marseilles. I have smelt this before in her room at Baskerville Hall. She has been forced to sit here, bound, naked, and no doubt gagged, then forced to suffer his abominations.'

'And the vulture, no doubt, has taken his prey with him,' observed Lestrade.

I felt a wave of nausea rise up from my stomach. What manner of monster defiles, then murders small children and tortures women? I could not even envisage it. This invisible foe leered at us through the stench and decay of the metropolis, goading us, leaving behind a growing tide of cruelty and devastation.

'I think that, for tonight, we have seen enough,' said Holmes.

'I agree, Mr Holmes. I shall post two plain clothes detectives at the back and front, just in case he returns,' said Lestrade, as we made our way back up the uneven stone steps.

'Although I do not think it is likely. He is too cunning for that,' replied Holmes, wearily. 'However, all is not lost.' He smiled and took from his coat pocket a crumpled white handkerchief. 'He has been careless. I found this on the cellar floor. It bears the monogram: JS.'

'Then we have more evidence that he was here. By the way, Mr Holmes, you may be interested to know that we had some success with evidence of the murders of the two telegraph boys.'

'Excellent. Something more than circumstantial evidence, I trust.'

'Our fingerprinting officer found two fingerprints we could not match to our criminal files department - which, by the way, has grown twice its size over the last year.'

'I am aware of it.'

'Well, it seems clear now that the murders may well have been committed by the same person.'

'Or the same person had attended and assisted both murders.'

'When we do arrest Stapleton, we shall be able to prove it either way.'

Chapter 14

DR WATSON'S DIARY 16th November 1901

I spent a restless night thinking about the horrors which Stapleton had committed, the fate of the two telegraph boys and the possible whereabouts of poor Beryl Baskerville. I wondered how any sane person could commit such abominable and detestable crimes. Like Holmes, I had read Krafft Ebbing's great study, Psychopathia Sexualis and I understood how sexual deviance can fuel violent tendencies, especially in men, but with Stapleton, there was an added dimension, a disturbing and manipulative maleficence which blighted the lives of all those who came into contact with him.

Holmes, who had clearly slept well if his cheerful manner was anything to go by, had already finished his breakfast and was smoking his old cherrywood at the table, his spent matches and dottles of shag tobacco strewn across the clean white cloth. I was reminded that at times he could be a most untidy man. However, I said nothing.
'You look as if you have not slept,' he observed.
'You are correct.'
'Then I am only sorry to have to hurry you, Watson, but we shall have to make an early start.'
'Why, where are we going?'
'We are going hunting.'
'Hunting Reynard?'

'No, bigger game than that. We shall be hunting Stapleton, who, so far, has eluded us, just like your Reynard. But today I shall set a dog to catch a dog, you may count on it. He shall not evade our attentions for much longer. But first, we shall visit our old friend Sherman in Pinchin Street.'

Pinchin Street. How the name resonated with me. On Tuesday 10th, September 1889, under a railway arch in Pinchin Street, a woman's torso had been discovered. No other body parts were found, despite a search of the area, and neither the victim nor the culprit were ever identified. Chief Inspector Swanson had visited the scene of the crime with Holmes and Holmes had observed that the presence of blood within the torso indicated that death was not from haemorrhage or cutting of the throat. The pathologist, however, had noted that the general bloodlessness of the tissues and vessels indicated that haemorrhage was the cause of death. Newspaper speculation that the body belonged to Lydia Hart, a local prostitute who had recently disappeared, was refuted after she was found recovering in hospital after "a bit of a spree". Another claim that the victim was a missing girl called Emily Barker was also refuted, as the torso was from an older and taller woman. The age of the victim was estimated at 30–40 years. Holmes had not considered this to be a Ripper case, and instead suggested a link to similar dismembered body cases in Rainham and Chelsea, as well as the 'The Whitechapel Murders'. These three murders and the Pinchin Street case were suggested to be the work of a serial killer, nicknamed the "Torso killer", who could either be the same person as "Jack the Ripper" or a separate killer of uncertain connection. However, behind Pinchin Street was Pinchin Lane.

At number 3 lay the delapidated shop premises of 'old Sherman.' Sherman was a grey bearded, aged taxidermist, who, thirty years ago, had emigrated to Britain, fleeing persecution from German anti-semitism. However, he had discovered that anti Jewish feelings in the East End of London were no less intense, and subsequently kept his religious beliefs and practices to himself. Sherman was an expert at his trade and could stuff virtually anything that was brought to him. He also dealt in the business of importing rare animals and birds from exotic climes. During the affair which I recorded in my published account as 'The Sign of Four,' I described how Holmes had used one of Sherman's dogs. Toby had proved to be an ugly, long-haired, lop-eared creature, half spaniel and half lurcher, brown and white in colour, with a very clumsy, waddling gait. But his sense of smell was singularly acute.

'Mr 'olmes, so very nice to see you. You are looking well. And you also, Doctor. 'Ow can I be of assistance to you both?'
'We have come to borrow Toby. Is he available?'
'Toby is no longer with us, Sadly, he passed away a month ago. I shall miss the little feller.'
'I am sorry to hear that. Do you have a dog with similar olfactory powers?'
'You mean do I have a good sniffer?'
'I do indeed.'

'I believe I've just the thing. His name is Caesar and he's a bloodhound. He's in one of the kennels. I shall go and fetch him for you, if you wish.'

Old Sherman disappeared into the back of his ramshackle shop and reappeared a few minutes holding on a strong leash a large bloodhound with unusually long, gangly legs and dewlaps.

'Caesar, meet Mr 'olmes,' said Sherman, pattting the hound's broad back.

'This fellow will meet our needs.'

'Cash up front, Mr 'olmes. How long d'you need him for?'

'At least a day. Hard to determine. I will give you two guineas as a deposit.'

'That'll do nicely. Can't offer you a macaw by any chance?'

'I am afraid not. Just the dog.' Holmes held out the two guineas. 'Come on, Caesar, I have a job for you!'

Number 26 Goulston Street was even more tawdry by the light of day and the presence of an emaciated beggar in the opening to the alleyway did nothing to enhance its appearance. We found a weary looking Lestrade leaning on the railings of the property, finishing a cigarette and giving instructions to a uniformed officer.

'Just get rid of him, Stevens,' I heard him exclaim, 'and tell him not to come back.'

He turned and smiled at the sight of the bloodhound.

'Ah, so this is your secret weapon, Holmes.'

'His name is Caesar.'

'Well, Caesar, let us see if you are up to a challenge.'

Caesar barked at Lestrade.
'You see, he understands every word I say!'
Caesar strained at his leash.
'I shall need something of Beryl Baskerville's,' said Holmes. 'Sit. Good boy.'
Holmes produced a small piece of meat from his greatcoat pocket and Caesar immediately devoured it.
'The dress we found in the basement.'
'That is exactly what we need.'

Lestrade instructed the constable to fetch the dress from the back of the Black Maria and Holmes knelt down with it, letting the dog sniff and paw at it. Then Caesar looked at Holmes with his large gentle eyes, ready to receive his instructions. A few seconds later, he was loping forwards on his long, bandy legs, nose to the ground.

We moved at speed through the busy streets, attracting some amused and curious onlookers in our wake. Down Wentworth Street we careered, across Brick Lane, then into Chicksand Street, Greatorex Street, Old Montagu Street, across Valiant Gardens, until at last we entered Durward Street, a narrow side road of two and three storey, yellow bricked houses, some of which looked neglected and in need of paint. Number twenty three was a three storey house with shutters behind the windows. Adjacent to the property and next to the fire escape, stood a semi derelict garage with double doors, painted a dingy green. Caesar came to an abrupt stop outside the house, cocked his head and sniffed. Then he dropped down and began sniffing and whining at the steps to the basement. Holmes pulled at the leash and whispered into Caesar's ear. The bloodhound obediently sat on its haunches, then lowered its head. Tying the leash to the railings, Holmes beckoned us.

'Lestrade, will you please cover the rear entrance. Watson and I shall take the front.'

Holmes drew out of his greatcoat two small bobby pins and inserted them into the lock. There was a soft click, then the front door opened slightly. I took out my revolver and followed him inside, barely daring to breathe. The hallway lay in darkness, owing to the closed shutters, and there was a rancid smell about the place. Slowly, we advanced into each of the downstairs rooms, stopping every so often to listen. Then we heard it, a slight creak in the floorboards above us.

'It is he, Watson,' whispered Holmes.

We climbed the stairs, placing our feet gingerly upon each step. We had almost reached the top of the staircase, when there was a sudden flash and crack as I felt the hot metal of a bullet pass by my head.

'Down, Watson, down!' Holmes urged me. He was onto the landing in a second, firing into the darkness. I stayed where I was, fearing the worst for my companion. Seconds passed and I could hear Holmes breathing as he lay in wait for his prey. Suddenly, the room was filled with light as a door at the rear of the room opened. From my vantage point I could see the outline of Stapleton as he lunged for the fire escape. But Holmes was on him like a tiger, pouncing on his prey. I watched, powerless to intervene, as the two men struggled with each other, Holmes raining blows on Stapleton's head, the latter swinging wildly at him. With a last, desperate swing, I watched as Stapleton staggered, lost his balance and then disappeared over the railing of the fire escape.

I joined my companion and, looking down, saw the motionless figure of Jack Stapleton, spreadeagled on the road below us, head enclosed by a pool of blood.
'It is over, Holmes.'
'Not quite over. We must now find Beryl Baskerville,' observed Holmes, cooly.

We did not have to wait long. When we descended the stairs, we discovered Lestrade at the top of the cellar stairs, accompanied by a uniformed constable and two other officers in the process of heaving Stapleton's shattered remains on a stretcher.

'Someone you should see, Mr Holmes,' Lestrade explained. Holmes nodded to the detective and silently, we made our way down the worn steps into an almost darkened dry cellar, measuring about fourteen by sixteen feet. On a leather backed chair, her head bowed, her black hair grimy and tousled, her naked torso partly covered by a policeman's jacket, sat Beryl Baskerville. She turned and smiled at Holmes.

'Thank God you have come at last,' she said, her eyes brimming with tears. 'Have you found him?'
'Stapleton is dead. He shall trouble you no more,' Holmes replied, sombrely.
'She has been sorely abused,' Lestrade turned away from her, speaking now in confidential tones to us.
'So I see. You see the weals on her wrists and her neck, Watson? He has bound her, beaten her, kept her captive here and subjected her to all manner of indignities.'
Lestrade beckoned to the constable. 'Take Mrs Baskerville here to the station, Staunton, and see that she is given some tea and a hot meal - and ask Sergeant Hawkins to bring a couple of extra lanterns in here, will you?'

We stood in the semi - darkness, each one of us silent and with his own thoughts about what we had seen. Sergeant Hawkins lit the lanterns he had brought in and soon the cellar was brightly lit. The perimeter of the room revealed a huge number of brown paper packages and files.
'What have we here?' asked Lestrade.
Holmes did not reply at first and busied himself for several minutes with opening and examining the packages. Then he turned to Lestrade. There are multiple copies here of almost every book published - and republished - by Leonard Smith. There are also manuals, certain 'devices', and a wide variety of photographic material. Some of the 'intimate portraits' here are of society ladies who I recognise - from their faces, I must add.' He reached for some of the black files stacked up on the rear wall and opened the first. There was a list of female names and London postal addresses. Some of these had a small

portrait attached to them, showing the 'best' features of the subject. 'Some of these are his drabs, Watson, but not all of them.'

I glanced at the photographs. Some showed their subjects sitting on a chair in a provocative pose, others seem to have been taken out of doors, with sea or woodland backdrops. The women were of all ages and not all of them were handsome. And as Holmes had correctly observed, some of them were undoubtedly celebrities. I recognised among them a marchioness, a leading contralto, a renowned actress, a cabinet minister's wife and a well known author of popular romances.

'He has had them all in his thrall,' observed Holmes. 'They either worked for his gang or were blackmailed by him. His roots went deep.'
'Ah, and here if I am not mistaken, inspector, is a list of his confederates with their contact details. This may be of use to you.'
'Indeed it will, Mr Holmes.' The inspector scanned the list. 'Several of these names are only too familiar to me. And here is Parker, our garotter.'
'So I see. But I am still curious to know the identity of our third murderer.'
'You are referring to the murder of Leonard Smith?'
'I am. Clearly, the ring leader was Stapleton himself for he was reported as tall and wearing a moustache - which fits Stapleton. But the third had a pony tail.'
'I shall have to cross reference the names on this list with our criminal records back at the Yard. I'll also see if we

can link the fingerprints taken at the scenes of crime regarding the telegraph boys.'

'Excellent. The net tightens, Watson.'

'And this afternoon, I shall ask Beryl Baskerville for a detailed statement regarding her abduction. I shall have an officer drop a copy into you in the morning, Mr Holmes.'

'I am grateful to you. Now, I believe we have had enough excitement for one day, Watson. I think lunch at Simpsons would be most appropriate.'

BERYL BASKERVILLE'S STATEMENT TO THE POLICE - 16th November 1901

I met Jack Stapleton when I was just sixteen. My parents, my two brothers and my older sister Dolores, all lived in a small, semi-derelict house in the suburbs of San Jose, the capital of Costa Rica, where my antecedents had lived for centuries. We were originally a farming family, but by the middle of the century we fell on hard times and my parents endured much poverty. I had managed to get a job as a cleaner in the Alta Hotel to the north of the city, which involved a four mile walk each day and I worked long hours for little pay.

Stapleton, who was a guest at the hotel, came across me one morning as I was cleaning his room. He spoke fluent Spanish and introduced himself as a traveller, photographer and journalist in his native England. I was at once impressed by his expensive clothes, his dashing appearance and charming manner. He had the most hypnotic eyes I have ever seen. When he asked me if I would like to join him for a drink in the hotel bar, I told him that it would be unwise, since I might be sacked for being seen in the company of a tourist, especially considering my age, so we went to one of the small bars in a backstreet in the La Merced area. I had never drunk alcohol before so it did not take long before I felt quite inebriated. Jack, who regaled me with his anecdotes and amusing stories, painted a rosy picture of England which immediately appealed to my sense of adventure. I imagined myself escaping to London with him and living a life of perpetual luxury instead of staying in Costa, enduring a poverty stricken existence and having to work my fingers to the bone in order to support my brothers and my ageing parents.

And that is exactly how things turned out. Jack Stapleton took me back to his room that very night and it was in that hot room on a Sunday evening that I lost my virginity. Although he was ruthless and quite remorseless in his dealings with other human beings, he was skilled in the art of love making and knew many ways to stimulate passion and desire in a woman. Until I met Stapleton I had not heard of such terms as *gamahuche* and a *menage a trois*, nor even thought what it meant to enact them. It is only a pity that he did not have a heart. Things might have been so different for both of us.

Jack was born under the sign of Scorpio. People born under Scorpio are renowned for being obsessively driven, resourceful, secretive, loyal, and passionate. Jack was all of these things and more. He loved sex for its own sake. It intoxicated him. It was like a drug for him. I consider myself to be a very passionate woman, but I could never catch up with Jack's demands. He would have intercourse with me at absolutely any time and anywhere, in a hotel room, in a park, in a hansom cab, in a back street, even in a graveyard. It excited him that others might see us or that we would run the risk of being arrested for public indecency. We were fortunate, I suppose, that we managed to avoid prosecution.

Jack was both an excellent linguist and a first rate photographer. When he lost his job as a journalist, working for The Times, he purchased a boy's preparatory school near Whitby and whilst he and another master taught, I acted as a matron to the pupils. Sadly, this was not a success and a boy died after Jack beat him so cruelly that the youth suffered a heart attack. We moved back to London, eager to avoid scandal and he boldly invested much of his remaining savings in a studio. We lived there for a number of years and gradually he began to prosper as portrait photography became more and more popular among the wealthy classes. One day, one of his female subjects asked Jack for a portrait of her posing naked and told him that she wanted it done as a gift to her husband. He obliged her and was paid handsomely for his labours. This spurred him into action, and, driven as he always was, he soon let it be known among certain sections of London society that he was open for business for this more intimate and discreet form of photography. Women - and men - from 'polite society' flocked to the studio, and I recognised among them many famous names including Oscar Wilde, the actress, Ann Sutherland, the model, Evelyn Nesbit, Isadora Duncan, the dancer, and Lillie Langtry. One of our clients was a member of the Royal Family, but all I shall say about the gentleman was that he was something of a lady's man.

It was whilst we were enjoying such success in London, that he was approached by the late Professor Moriarty. I was never quite certain of their precise relationship, but I do know that it involved the production of certain books, photographs and magazines of an erotic nature, which were then proving popular among the upper classes, especially those who had taken holidays in 'gay Paris.' Jack was introduced to a publisher whose name was Leonard Smith, a publisher of erotica, who also ran an exclusive book club. However, the two men later fell out because of a dispute over certain business issues which he did not share with me. Later on I learned that Smith had been murdered.

In the year that followed, I saw less and less of Jack - who was never my husband in legal terms, by the way - and it was only through a female friend that I discovered he had been given responsibility by the Professor for the management of most of the London bawdy houses. This new post made us comparatively wealthy and Jack decided that we should move to the country, leaving his photographic business in the hands of a colleague called Parker.

The Baskerville Papers

We decided to buy a house on Dartmoor where Jack could enjoy his study of butterflies - he was always something of a collector, both of insects and women - and it was there that he explained to me the nature of his plan regarding the inheritance of the Baskerville fortune. He had delved into his ancestry and was astonished to learn that, once Sir Charles died, there were only two direct successors to the family fortune - a Canadian by the name of Henry Baskerville and himself. He enlisted my support and also that of a woman called Laura Lyons, a woman of somewhat loose morals whom he had previously had an affair with in London. I soon struck up a friendship with Laura, who was actually a delightful and loving woman and together we set up The Womens' Mission.

As you already know, learning of the Baskerville curse, and discovering that Sir Charles suffered a heart condition, Jack decided to make the legend a fearful reality, purchased a hound and brought the creature down on the London train, then kept it in one of the old disused mines. He learned to cultivate Sir Charles' friendship and made frequent visits to the hall where he endorsed the veracity of the 'hell hound' legend. He also encouraged Sir Charles to arrange a series of so called 'soirees', which were nothing more than orgies for wealthy people as far afield as Exeter, the key to the popularity of these events being 'discretion.' Jack could be very discreet when it suited his needs.

Unfortunately for Jack, his plan failed, due mainly to the efforts of Mr Sherlock Holmes. And I had thought never to see him again. To be frank, I was relieved about this turn of events. Jack had grown increasingly violent to me during this period and his appetite for sex had become perverse. He insisted that I should be 'punished' prior to our having intercourse. This began with heavy spanking, then degenerated into a variety of cruel looking whips which left me sore and bruised. He would also delight in tying me to a pole in the lounge where he would beat me soundly before ravishing me. When he learned that Sir Henry and I were deeply in love, he was consumed by jealousy. I had never seen such anger. He treated me cruelly, whipping me for almost an hour with a bull whip until I begged him for mercy.

You may imagine my astonishment when I discovered that he had not died in the Grimpen Mire after all but had survived the ordeal and returned briefly to London where he sought refuge with the aid of Parker and the Moriarty gang, thus changed his appearance.

I had taken my usual route across the moor on a bright September morning. As I approached one of the ancient hut dwellings I heard someone moving about inside. When he emerged alongside a shorter, older man, I barely recognised Jack for he was sporting a thick moustache, his hair was dyed black and had been cut short and he seemed slightly older. The older man was bald and tattooed with a cruel mouth and teeth which were yellow and broken.

'Surprised to see me?' he asked, smiling at me.

I said nothing, fearing the worst.

'Time to pay your debts, Beryl,' he snarled.

I started running back down the track but the big man caught me and pulling me down, pushed a wad soaked in chloroform onto my mouth. I lost consciousness and only came to when I was at the railway station, where I struggled in vain to free myself. But the big man placed the wad over my mouth again and I was bundled unconscious into a first class compartment.

I remember little else about the journey to London but only recall being taken from a cab and marched down a narrow flight of stairs into a dark cellar where I remained for several days. What followed was beyond my worst imaginings. Stapleton possessed an inventive if perverse mind and had equipped the room with a portable mechanism whose purpose I could not at first divine. Later I was to learn the depths to which his disordered mind had sunk. In the middle of the room he had erected two wooden pillars. Between each of the pillars that supported the ceiling hung a pair of strong rope-pulleys working on a roller mechanism concealed in the beams and actuated by electricity. Should Stapleton want me to remain upright, he had simply to attach the ropes to my wrists, and my arms would be pulled straight up and well over my head, thus forcing me to stand erect, and at the same time rendering my body defenceless and at his mercy. The pillars themselves could be utilized as whipping posts, being provided with rings to which I could be fastened in such a way that I could not move at all. All the ropes and straps were fitted with swivel snap-hooks. To attach them to my limbs, Stapleton used an endless band of the strongest and softest silk rope. It was an easy matter to slip the band (doubled) round my wrist or ankle, pass one end through the other and draw tight, then snap the free end into the swivel hook. No amount of plunging or struggling would loosen this attachment, and the softness of the silk prevented my delicate flesh from being rubbed or even marked.

I stayed in that cellar for what seemed like weeks, often unable to move at all, subject to his every whim and caprice. I never knew when he was coming, nor when I might be freed. And by this means, he gradually broke my will. I became his slave, and learned to obey his every command. I became his mute and obedient accomplice in many of his abominable crimes, even accompanying him in the luring and murder of those poor telegraph whose tragic ends I was forced to witness. The memory of those butchered boys haunts me even now.

It had been Stapleton's intention to kill Henry by subtle means. At first he sent a prostitute called Sophie Richards to work as a maid at the Hall. She was to seduce him and introduce into his meals a little known substance which he had obtained from the native Indian tribes when he was travelling in South America. Its effects were to induce extreme paranoia and hallucinations in the subject, coupled with an increase in libido. The plan was to gradually unhinge him so utterly that he would lose his mind and eventually be committed to an asylum. Richards was to visit him in the asylum and then poison him using a substance known as Bufodienolide - a secretion from toad skin which was also an aphrodisiac which, when taken regular amounts caused heart failure. My abduction and incarceration would provide the opportunity for Richards to marry Henry prior to his death and thus provide a means for Stapleton to access his immense wealth, using an assumed identity. What fate might eventually befall me was never discussed and I feared to dwell on it, but I knew that my demise would be necessary for his plan to succeed. Meanwhile I was be his plaything and accomplice.

I knew of this much because he would often come to me and tell me of such dark matters before abusing me, in order to augment my pain. And causing limitless pain to others was what often motivated him. Although he never confided in me regarding the murder of Sophie Richards, I suspect that he ordered her death since she had grown too close to Henry and may even have fallen in love with him. I cannot be sure of which.

I know nothing about his involvement with the Fenians since he never mentioned it but I do recall some men speaking in Irish accents above me on the ground floor on more than one occasion.

The Baskerville Papers

Chapter 15

DOCTOR WATSON'S JOURNAL February 20th, 1924

And that, I imagined, was the end of the matter which I have decided to call 'The Baskerville Affair.' Beryl Baskerville's statement explained everything which the police needed to know except for the precise details of the Fenian outrage. But I noticed that, far from being satisfied with the results of the case, Holmes seemed ill at ease over the days that followed Stapleton's demise.
'Something is amiss, Watson,' explained Holmes as we sat smoking our after dinner pipes on a cold November evening. 'Yet I cannot for the life of me figure out what it is.'
'It will reveal itself to you in time. You must be patient.'
'I think that I have never been quite the same since that ordeal at the Reichenbach Falls. I seem to lack my former mental acuity.'
'Nonsense, Holmes, you are as sharp as ever.'

And there the conversation came to an abrupt conclusion. Holmes retired to the privacy of his bedroom and I saw nothing more of him until the following morning when, at around eight, there was a ring of the doorbell. I heard the tread of heavy footsteps on our stairs.
'That is undoubtedly Lestrade,' commented Holmes. 'Flat footed. I wonder what brings him here so early in the day.'
'Glad to find you both up and about,' said the inspector as my companion beckoned him to a chair. I raked the hot

embers of the fireplace and loaded on fresh coal as Holmes relit his old clay.

'What is it, Lestrade?'

'We finally managed to match those two fingerprints I mentioned to you a while ago - the prints from the murder weapons used to butcher the telegraph boys.'

'Excellent work. And?'

'As you may already know, we had no record of Stapleton's prints or of Beryl Baskerville's - the latter was fingerprinted only yesterday as a matter of routine, since she was an important witness to the murders but claimed she was merely an unwilling onlooker. It turns out that both Stapleton and she left matching prints on both of the knives used to butcher the two boys. And there was something else we discovered.'

'And, pray, what is that?'

'You may recall that when we visited Leonard Smith's flat, we found a smashed mirror?'

'I recall it.'

'When we examined it more closely at the Yard, we found a partial hand and thumb print. The print matches that of Beryl Baskerville.'

Holmes leapt to his feet.

'I have been a fool, Watson, an utter fool!' he exclaimed. 'I saw the evidence but I failed to observe it!'

'With respect, Mr Holmes, I wouldn't say that was true. You could not have known about the recent forensic evidence.'

'The third person seen by the occupant of flat 2.'

'Mrs Gilmore.'
'Yes, Smith's neighbour. She described the third man as being short in stature and wearing a pony tail. But it wasn't a man at all. It was a woman, and a highly dangerous one.'
'You intend to arrest her?' I enquired of Lestrade, as Holmes began striding up and down the room, agitatedly.
'There's little point in it, since the evidence is largely circumstantial.'
'But surely, the fingerprints -' I protested.
'They merely prove that Beryl was at the scene of those crimes. It would take a great deal more than that to convince a jury that she is guilty of murder,' said Holmes. 'No, we need something more substantial. Her statement to the police would suggest she was a victim in these crimes. She had no choice but to serve as Stapleton's accomplice. But what if her statement is substantially untrue? How would even the best barrister prove that? No, Watson, it simply will not suffice.'
Holmes re-lit his pipe, his face like thunder. There was a light knock on the door and Holmes opened it to reveal Mrs Hudson, holding a telegram.

'I got this just now, Mr Holmes. It's marked urgent and needs a reply.'
'Thank you, Mrs Hudson.'
Holmes opened the telegram.
'What does it say?' asked Lestrade.
'It's from Bovey Tracey. *Sir Henry dead. Suspicious circumstances. Maid in custody. Would appreciate assistance. Merrivale.* Just one minute, Mrs Hudson whilst I write a reply. There. Please see that this is sent

immediately. Watson, look up the time of the next train from Paddington to Exeter. Where is Beryl Baskerville now, Lestrade?'

'She is staying at the Northumberland Hotel, Charing Cross, for a few days whilst she recuperates.'

'Then we shall need to question her again.'

' I shall contact the hotel immediately.'

'The Exeter train leaves from Paddington in forty minutes. It's an express.'

'Thank you Watson. Now, Lestrade, Watson and I need a cab.'

It was just after midnight when Holmes and I at last reached Baskerville Hall. As was often the case on Dartmoor, the Hall was shrouded in swirling mist out of which the Edison lamps in the driveway glowed like sentinels. We were ushered inside by a lugubrious Barrymore to find Inspector Merrivale in the lounge. He seemed tired and agitated.

'Thank you for being so prompt, Mr Holmes. The body is upstairs.'

'You have not moved it?'

'Only the doctor has examined Sir Henry's body. According to Barrymore here, he had been ill for some while and was experiencing hallucinations.'

'Let me see the body.'

We climbed the stairs to the main bedroom where Barrymore lit an oil lamp, then pulled back the bedsheet.

'Tell me what happened,' said Holmes.

'Sir Henry ate dinner and about an hour later started having severe cramps. He kept complaining that he was being attacked by demons,' Barrymore informed us. 'He tried to jump out of the window but we managed to restrain him. He died in terrible pain. It is all very sad, especially since Beryl was coming down to be reunited with him tomorrow.'

Holmes leaned over the body and sniffed.
'It is as I thought. He has been poisoned with Bufodienolides. He has absorbed a great deal of it and it has destroyed his nervous system.'
'I have never heard of this poison.'
'The more common name is toad skin. It is popular in some South American countries as an aphrodisiac but when used in large quantities it is positively lethal. You say you have the maid, Lucy, in custody, inspector?'
'For now, yes, but I shall need proof of her complicity if I wish to charge her.'
'Quite so, Then let us first examine her room.'

But again, Holmes' attempt to bring a case against the Stapleton dynasty was doomed to failure. A search of the maid's room yielded but one clue: a letter from an employment agency in London informing Lucy that she had been offered a post at Baskerville Hall, following a most satisfactory reference from her previous employers, a *Mr and Mrs Vandeleur.* Subsequent enquiries informed us that the Vandeleurs also provided a reference for the unfortunate Sophie Richards.

As for Beryl Baskerville, she too evaded justice. Having been apprehended by Lestrade's officers she was put into a Black Maria and taken to Scotland Yard for questioning. There she remained in custody for the next two days, refusing to change her statement or admit her complicity in any of the five murders. On the morning of the third day she was found dead in her cell, having swallowed a cyanide pill.

Holmes never again referred to The Baskerville Affair, as he termed it, and I avoided making any reference to it thereafter. So the Baskerville papers remained in my old despatch box, consigned to oblivion. The case could never have been brought into the public domain, so dreadful and shocking were its contents. Besides, some of the names of those involved in Stapleton's empire were among the most exalted in the land. Looking back now, I feel I was not wrong in keeping my confidence, for this case, more than any other dealt with by Holmes during our long association, revealed the widespread moral corruption that infested our society. And more alarming, perhaps, is the fact that such corruption has grown even greater after the turn of the new century. Today, as I write this addendum, I note from the Press that child prostitution is more rampant than ever, and the pornography industry thrives like never before both in film and printed matter. In Soho, London, where every other house is a brothel and sodomites advertise themselves on street corners, every possible perversity can be satisfied if the price is right.

As for Holmes he was never the same after the case concluded and soon fell into a deep depression. For once in his career he had come up against a foeman worthy of his steel and it had found him wanting. So the Baskerville Affair shall remain, as a shadow that threatened to blight so many lives, its memory now banished to the darkness of oblivion.

Also by the same author:

Sherlock Holmes: The Plagues Of London

… The Baskerville Papers

The Baskerville Papers

The Baskerville Papers

The Baskerville Papers

The Baskerville Papers

Made in the USA
Middletown, DE
27 November 2016